# Voodoo Child

Death is not the final journey

R.D. McKown

authorHOUSE®

*AuthorHouse™*
*1663 Liberty Drive*
*Bloomington, IN 47403*
*www.authorhouse.com*
*Phone: 1 (800) 839-8640*

*Published by AuthorHouse    01/05/2017*

*ISBN: 978-1-5246-5816-8 (sc)*
*ISBN: 978-1-5246-5815-1 (e)*

*Print information available on the last page.*

*This book is printed on acid-free paper.*

# Chapter One

The two boy scouts, ages twelve, and eleven, were searching the dark woods for firewood for their camp. It was getting darker out, they starting hurrying along, looking for some sticks. One of them, Ben, spied a stack of wooden sticks heavily piled together. They were a little long, but he could break them up. The eleven year old looked at Ben. "Let's hurry up", he suggested, looking around. "Fraid of the dark, sissy" Ben said, jokingly. "There could be bears around here", Jim the eleven years old, replied, rubbing his hands together. "Well help me then", Ben stated, starting to gather up some of the wood sticks. Jim reluctantly began helping Ben. Half way down, Ben straightened up, startled. "Oh, Shit!" he exclaimed. "What? Jim asked, "Is it a snake? "Hell no! Ben, replied, his face ashen, his body started to shake. He moved to one side of the wood. A shriveled hand poked obscenely out of the wood, its fingers pointing aimlessly at the sky. They both screamed, and ran back to the camp. The scoutmaster and half a dozen troops were opening up their tents, some struggling with it harder than others. Ben and Jim came crashing to the encampment, gasping for air, their heart beats gaining volume. "What the hell! The scoutmaster Gene, looked at the two irritatingly "What's' going on", he asked the two, rubbing dirt off his hands. Jim smelled something bad on Ben. Damn, he thought, Ben had shit his pants! Who's the sissy now? He thought. Ben terrified to speak pointed to the woods. Jim gathered himself together, and said, "There's a body in the woods". Gene stared at them incredulously. "This better not be a joke", Gene growled at them. Ben sat down, petrified. "I'll take you there", Jim said, pointing to the woods. They came across the woodpile, the hand sticking out, and the fingers pointing skyward. It was getting darker now. Gene produced a flashlight, illuminating the area. Gene bent over with his free left hand, holding the light. He touched the hand. The hand came alive, gripping Genes' hand. Gene shocked, tried to loosen its grip. He fell to his knees, wanting to yell. A voice screamed out from the woodpile" *Anwe*" the female voice screamed. Then the hand collapsed. Jim, staring, produced a cell phone. He dialed 911. A voice responded, "911, what's your emergency? "You're not going to believe this shit! He said to the operator. The operator listened, and said, "Is this a joke! Jim shook Gene out of his shock, and gave him the phone. Gene, a little dazed, but more together now, gave the operator the information. "Ambulance and sheriffs are on their way. Stay where you are so we can find you". Annie Lecroux jerked to awareness when the phone rang. She had just finished her last case, Albert Grunaman, the ritualistic killer. It had been twenty-four hours since she slept. Rubbing the sleep out of her eyes, she glanced at the small clock sitting on her bedside table. Eight p.m.! She had been asleep only two hours! Clad only in a white t-shirt, and rainbow colored panties, she padded across the room, to grab the phone on her front room wall. Picking it up, she said sleepily, "Hello who is it? A voice replied on the phone, "Annie, sorry to wake you, I know you haven't had much sleep, "Neither have I". It was Billy Walker, her newest partner in the Homicide Division. "What . . . What is it", she asked, slight irritation in her voice. "Hated to bother you, but we caught a case out in Briarwood Forrest. "And.., she paused." It looks like another weird one, a ritual thing". He hesitated, waiting for her answer. "Can I pick you up in say . . . thirty minutes." "O.K.", she sighed, mumbling to herself. She continued, "I'm going to take a quick shower and cleanup. "See you in a few". She hung up. "Damn!" she remarked. Stripping off her t-shirt and panties, heading for the shower. She stepped into the bathroom, turning on the jets to the shower. She adjusted the heat, just right! Enjoying the warmth, she relaxed, scrubbing herself. Shampooing her hair, then she rinsed off. She turned the shower off, stepped out, and grabbed a towel from a plastic rack next to the shower. A full length mirror was displayed on the back of the bedroom door. Her medium length hair, jet black, hung wetly on her shoulders. She made a quick exam of herself. Her breasts were firm, and her nipples were dark, erect, and almost purple in color. She stood about 5 foot seven, and one hundred and twenty five pounds. Still keeping my weight down, she thought. That surprised her, considering the amount of doughnuts, and fast food she had eaten, during her stint as a detective, second grade. Quickly drying off, she went into the bedroom, to find something to wear. Looking in the closet, she produced a pair of tight blue jeans, black t-shirt, and her flats. She clipped her badge to her jeans, and entered the front room to wait on Billy. A knock on the door announced his arrival. Opening the door, Billy stood there, grinning, with two hot cups of coffee in his hands. "You sure know how to help a gal out", Annie said, smiling. "Hi there", he said, handing her a Styrofoam cup. Annie took it, and stepped back to let him enter. She looked Billy over. Medium length blonde hair, six foot two, and about two hundred pounds. What a hunk, she thought, a blush appearing slightly on the cheeks of her face. Billy trying not to stare gave Annie a quick going over. Annie's coco colored skin, her nipples protruding nicely through her t—shirt. Almost a welcome sign! Billy felt a surge of arousal in him. "Forget something? He asked, sheepishly. Annie looked down, seeing she had forgotten her bra. "Damn it", she said, blushing again, "I'll be right back". Annie took off her t-shirt in the bedroom, grabbed a bra, and slipped it on. Replacing her t-shirt, she observed her tangled hair. She reached into a drawer, producing a hard brush, and worked the tangles out. She went into the bathroom, looking in a mirror, giving it a final brush. She grabbed some red lipstick, and applied it. Guess that will do, it's not like I'm going out on a date, she thought. Satisfied with her look, she returned to the front room. Billy was sitting on her brown leather couch, His immaculate grey Armani suit, and blue tie, fit him perfectly. Annie sighed; having a relationship with partner was bad business, no matter how he looked. Annie felt a twinge of regret. They had never broached the subject, but she could feel the physical tension in the air. They say Haitians have a sixth sense of these things. Annie was half Haitian, with a touch of Irish in her. Annie had been adopted by a French couple, who belonged to Doctors without Borders. The Lecrouxs had been in Haiti, setting up an emergency hospital in her village. Annie, when she was about five, was found wandering the streets of her small village. She looked filthy, raggedy, and tired. She also looked malnourished, and in shock. Doctors Henry Lecroux, and his wife, Madeline, had taken her in, restored her health, and having no children of their own, decided to adopt her. DNA testing had established her heredity. The Lecrouxs were exceptional parents, and doted on Annie.

She had traveled to many different places with them. Brazil, Columbia, France. They had decided to settle down in the good old USA, For Annie's' upbringing. She was ten then, raised in New York. She attended NYU, with a major in Criminal Justice, and a minor in Haitian studies.

She spoke Haitian slang like a native. She had worked with NYPD for three years, and then transferred out to a small town in California, hoping for a more peaceful, easy post. Her parents were not pleased that she did that leaving for the west coast, but accepted her decision. They could see that the grind at NYPD was getting to her. But somehow, being Haitian, she wound up investigating serial killers, and ritualistic murders. She seemed to have a knack for it, finding the perpetrators. Annie looked at Billy. Billy came from a typical middle class family. An only child of a plumber, and a housewife. His parents had encouraged him to get an education. Cleaning crappers wasn't his idea of making a living. After high school, Billy joined the Marines, and was shipped to Afghanistan. He had seen some horrible things there! When his hitch was up, after three years, he left to attend his hometown community college. After graduating, he joined up with the local sheriffs' department, and the rest was history. Annie said to Billy, "Are we ready to go? Billy nodded, Billy had been on the force now, for eight years, and was recently promoted to detective. He stood up, and opened the door for Annie. Annie locked her door, and they descended down the stairs to the parking lot. Billy's car, an old beat up Crown Victoria, faded black, was there. The sheriffs' department obviously wasn't very good about new cars in their budget. Annie and Billy got in, and Billy fired up the old car. The starter grinded, then with a short back blast from it, they drove off. "Where is it? ", Annie asked him, as they cruised along. "A couple of miles in the San Bernardino mountains", he replied. "Well out to the boonies for me", said Annie sighing in resignation. It took them an hour before they reached the location. There it was! The ambulance parked on a hill, its red lights flashing, illuminating the darkness. The CSI, in their white van, parked next to it. As the two got out, they spotted Bud Kline, the coroner, up the hill. CSI had spread the yellow crime scene tape around one hundred feet in a circular area around it. As they trudged up the hill, they saw Bud examining the prone body of a female. Rocks grated on their shoes, as they approached. They stopped, on the left side of Bud, glancing at the body. Bud, short, bald, and in his fifties, glanced up at them. "Here's a weird one for you", he said, pointing at the body on the ground. "What the hell!' Annie exclaimed. The female body looking Haitian by descent, by a quick glance, had her two feet removed! It appeared to be surgically done, no ragged edges, a professional job. Billy gawked at the sight. "Guess he didn't want her to runaway, Bud smirked. He continued, "Maybe I should have done that to my ex-wife". "Not even funny you perv'", Annie admonished him. "Sorry", Bud said, standing up from the body. "I'll get her to autopsy, but by the looks of it, she slowly bled to death out here, after the amputation". Bud continued on," She's only been dead maybe ninety minutes, according to her core temp in her liver".

Bud stated further, "She was barely alive, when the boy scouts found her". "I'll need to talk to them ", Billy said. A uniformed deputy stood behind them. He spoke up, "Well one of them is here". The other ones' parents took him home to clean up, because he shit his pants", the officer said, trying to look serious. "All right", Annie spoke up, she turned to Billy, "You talk to the one that's here, and I'll go talk to boys' parents'. Billy nodded, and then took off towards the scout camp. The CSI approached Bud and Annie. "Damndest thing! He mumbled out loud to himself. "What? Asked Annie, looking at him. "No footprints, almost zero fibers, trace evidence". "Ridiculous!' Bud said, "Crimes always leave something behind". Bud continued, did you go over everything" The CSI gave him a glare, looking insulted. "I've been a CSI for twelve years, but I've never seen anything like this! Bud shrugged his shoulders, as Annie looked on amazed. "Great ", she said, "This is going to be a tough one". Annie went down the hill, her shoes clacking on the gritty dirt, to flag down a deputy, who sat bored, sitting in his patrol car. She walked up to the passenger window that was rolled half way down. "Take me to 333 Oregon drive, deputy, and "she said. The deputy nodded, and then thought to himself, Wonderful! Now I'm a chauffeur for the detectives! He shrugged, and then started up the car. They headed down the road, Annie lost in thought. Billy had made his way down to the scout camp. Billy spied Gene, the scoutmaster, and Jim. They were getting ready to board a putrid yellow bus. The camp had been dismantled, and packed away, into silver Humvee. "Hold it! Billy yelled, "Police officer". He flashed his badge at them. Gene and Jim halted their departure. Billy moved towards the two. "I need you to answer some questions", Billy said, clipping his badge back on his belt. The two, leader and scout, stood still, awaiting

Billy's' instructions. "What happened here? Billy asked. The two took turns explaining what they found. They explained about finding the woman. She was half alive, and then lay still, still gripping Genes' hand. "What did she say . . . anything", Billy inquired. "Omwe", "Or something like that". Billy pondered, must be some kind of foreign language, or nonsense, from a dying woman. Billy thanked the two, and then told them to give him their phone and address information. The two left on the bus, a small backfire coming from its tailback, then chugged along. Billy wondered, "What the hell is going on", he said to himself. Annie arrived at Ben's parent's house. She knocked softly, but firmly on the door. Ben's mother, an attractive blonde in her middle thirties, answered the door. Annie flashed her badge, the mom, introduced herself. "I'm Ben's mom, Georgia". She looked about nervously. "Please come in, quickly". She continued, as Annie stepped in" "I need you help! Annie moved quietly in, as Georgia moved to the side. Annie drew her nine millimeter kel-tech from her side holster, just in case. "In the kitchen, Hurry! Georgia exclaimed, pointing the way.

Annie moved swiftly into the kitchen area. Pots, pans, and food were scattered about the the kitchen, like some crazy abstract painting. Annie spied Ben in the corner. He stood near the refrigerator, his lips drawn back tight, eyes bulging out, brandishing a ten inch butcher knife. He was waving it around in the air, screaming at the top of his lungs. "What the . . ., Annie began, taking in the bizarre scene. Then Ben moved slowly towards her. Annie gripped her pistol tight. Please God, she thought, I don't want to shoot a child. Ben suddenly stopped moving, about three feet from her. A screeching, howling noise emitted from his mouth. "Maga, Maga, *Anwe, Anwe*", *the voice screamed.* It was not his voice! It sounded foreign, and feminine. Annie stared in shock. Ben dropped the knife, shuddered, and convulsed, and vomited twice a foul smell like something dead, He spun around in a circle twice, like a weird dance routine, and collapsed with a thud onto the kitchen floor. Georgia ran over to him. Annie holstered her gun, relieved. "Jesus", Annie murmured, "What the hell was that!

# Chapter Two

Billy's cell rang, while he was driving. He pulled over to the side of the road, here", he announced. It was Annie explaining the situation. Billy could hardly believe his ears. "Damn", he said into his cell. "Where are you now? Annie explained she was at the county hospital with Ben and Georgia. "On my way", Billy hung up. He restated the vehicle, turned on his red light, and raced to the hospital. It took him only thirty minutes to get there. He was going seventy, eighty miles an hour, weaving and dodging through traffic. Billy arrived in front of the hospital, slamming on his brakes. Several medical techs, who were unloading a patient on a gurney, glared at him. Billy flashed his badge at them. He had parked in a loading zone. The med techs, stood aside, as Billy rushed through the double hospital doors. Entering the corridor he looked about. There was a nurse, in her white uniform, approaching him. Billy flashed his badge. "Where? He asked her, mentioning Annie's' name, and Ben. "Room 1312, down the hall, and to your right. ", the nurse replied, her eyes wide as she inspected his badge. Billy hurried down the hallway. The nurse gazed at him, "Nice butt", she grinned, talking low. The nurse, Alicia, sighed, and continued on her rounds. Billy had turned right in the hallway. He noticed the room number, and entered. There say Annie, in a fold out chair. The mother he guessed was bending over the child in the bed. The boy, had restraints on both arms, and IV's, in them. "Annie? Asked Billy, soaking up the scene. "Hi Billy", she stood up. Annie filled in Billy about the incident in detail. "The voice . . . the voice", she said, "It sounded less human, but feminine". "Schizo? He asked her, looking at the bed. "No history of it in his medical history". She continued, "A complete clean history, no alcohol, drug, or mental health issues. Mmm", Billy murmured. "Then what? Annie asked Billy to step out into the corridor. "Hear me out", Annie paused, touching his shoulder. Billy stood to listen attentively. "Demonic possession! She stated, looking people square in the eye. Billy rolled his eyes. "Come on, now", he smiled at her. "Listen to me", Annie raised her voice a little. "It fits the foreign language, his behavior, and the body without any trace evidence. She gripped his shoulder, tighter now. "Easy", Billy said, touching her hand that was on his shoulder. "I've seen this before, when I went on a tour of Haiti." She shivered. "This is black magic, evil". "Even if I believed, what should we do? Billy asked, "Call an exorcist? Billy attempted his poker face at her. Annie retorted, "The boy said something . . . Maga, Maga, *anwe*". "What the hell is that? Billy asked. Annie shrugged her shoulders, "A name . . . a name I think. She continued, "*Anwe*, is Haitian for help. "So its voodoo ritual stuff", Billy commented. "Maybe . . ." she said something even stronger. ""Like what? Billy asked again. "Don't know", Annie replied, shaking her head. Annie released Billy's' shoulder, much to his relief. Damn woman, had a strong grip! Billy rubbed his arm. "Sorry, Billy", she said, "I get carried away some times". "No doubt", he said, circulation returning to his arm. The nurse Alicia was making her rounds, when a sudden dizziness came upon her. She sat down in a chair next to a corridor. Must be fatigue, she thought. Short of help, she had been doing double shifts lately. Her head started spinning, and then she vomited some bile on the floor twice. The sound of heavy drumming pounded her ears. A voice spoke above the roar. "Finish it! Finish it! Room 1312! Alicia stood up, and went into the med room. She found a syringe, and injected it with FENTANYL, from an ampoule. Turning around, she exited, and moved slowly, like in a day dream, towards 1312. Billy and Annie were standing outside the room, discussing the two cases. They observed Alicia going into the room. Annie stared at her. "Something's wrong with her! She exclaimed to Billy. Billy peeked in. The mom was screaming, wrestling with the nurse, who was holding a syringe in her hand. Annie and Billy rushed in to grapple the nurse. The three of them struggled with the nurse, trying to remove the syringe from her right hand. The trio shuffled, and slid across the newly waxed floor, like some crazy barn room dance. Then Annie spoke to her, whispering. "Release Her! She commanded. Annie moved her hand in a circular motion, still hanging on with her right hand. Annie whispered something else to the nurse's ear, very faintly. Billy could not hear it.

The nurse stopped struggling, dropped to the ground with a thud, and released the syringe from her hand. Billy grabbed the syringe from the floor, and secured it. The nurse sat, her eyes bulging! She vomited a nasty smelling green substance on the floor. She spoke tonelessly to them, in a male voice. "Interfering with me!" "You all will die!" She glances up at Annie. Especially you, white witch!" Then the nurse collapsed, and began convulsing, then lay still. Billy said, breathing hard, "What the fuck was that? He looked at Annie, perplexed. Annie shook off the dread that was slowly creeping up on her. "A bokar", she said, shaking, Black magic, very evil! Billy stared at the scene, almost in shock. The mom hovered over her son. Billy shook his head in disbelief. "I must be losing my mind", he mumbled to himself. Billy called up a police unit. Then he quickly put the cuffs on Alicia, still unconscious. Billy was taking no chances. After calming down Ben's mom, he took Annie over to the side. "I can't believe this shit, but it must be true", he said to her. Believe it! Annie said "We must find out who's doing this". "Our lives could be in jeopardy", she concluded, "Especially Me! "What did he call you . . . ? White witch, but your dark skinned Haitian", he commented. Annie returned, "It's a term for a practice of good magic, a good witch, or Mambo". "I'll explain later", she said in a very low voice. Two uniformed officers appeared at the door. "Take her in", Billy said, pointing to the nurse on the floor. "She's out", commented the shorter officer. "Don't trust that, Billy remarked, "Arrest her for attempted murder". The taller officer, shrugged, and the two picked her up, half carrying her through the door. Annie and Billy decided to return to the office, and make out a report. They checked with the doctor about Ben, and he sent another nurse to check on him. Billy called again to the office. "I want another officer posted at a patients' room", he said to the dispatcher. He gave the dispatcher the info, and then hung up. Annie looked at Billy. "Sending an officer to watch over Ben", Billy said to her. Annie nodded in agreement. "We can wait till he gets here, then leave", She said, sitting back in a chair. She watched Ben and his mom closely.

Driving fast, with their red lights flashing, the two officers were on the way to book Alicia. Suddenly she sat up, glaring at them, pulling on her handcuffs. "No where to go, woman", the tall officer said. Alicia smiled viciously at them. "You want to see something? She asked, looking at the two officers. The short one in the passenger seat, turned around. Somehow she had slipped out of her uniform, and sat exposed in her bra and panties. "Holy shit! Exclaimed the short one. "", Abracadabra", she grinned, and her undergarments came off, without her touching them. "What the fuck? ", the tall one asked, taking a quick glance in the back seat. "Mama just needs a little love, honey", she said. She sprang forward, and with amazing strength, she tore the back screen of the car off. As she reached for the tall one driving, he grunted in surprise. She wrapped her arms around the man's 'neck, and stuck her tongue into his ear. "Give me some of that, honey she cackled. She twisted his head completely around, breaking it. "Oh shit . . . Oh shit! The short one said, trying to reach for his weapon. Alicia gave a high pitched laugh, and then grabbed the steering wheel. As the short one removed his pistol, aiming at her, he looked up. A yellow tour bus loomed ahead! S he aimed to fire at her, they rear ended the bus. At seventy miles an hour, the police car crumpled with a large crash, scattering debris all over the street. Shards of metal flew through the air, breaking shop windows. A woman carrying a bag of groceries was struck in the head by flying glass, her head exploded like a ripe watermelon. A shop owner stepping out to see what was going on, was disemboweled by the patrol cars, grill. The impact tipped the bus sideways, careening into the sidewalk, where it killed two more, which froze at the sight. The short cop was killed on impact, being thrown through the front window, shattered glass shredding him, as body parts, descended on to the ground, mixing it in with blood and asphalt. Alicia was thrown clear, and landed on the sidewalk she sprang up, holding her injured arm, and wiped the blood away from her face, with some broken glass still clinging to her hair. Naked, she darted down an alley way, to catch her breath. A crowd had gathered around the spectacle. Some people rushed forward, to help the passengers off the bus. The bus somehow, had righted itself, with help from the crowd. Several others ran to the police car to see if there was anything they could do. One of the people, commented in his high pitched voice, a teen wearing his headphones, giggled. "Jesus they all looked like Swiss cheeses". Then he bent over, vomiting on the ground, shaking. Several people turned away from the scene, almost dropping their cookies on the floor. Police cars came careening up to a halt, red lights flashing, illuminating the bizarre scene. Some people were still helping the passengers off the bus, while others made a vain attempt with a blanket they had found, covering the two mangled bodies. Two officers got out of their patrol car, and started putting up yellow crime scene tape around the area. Lieutenant McCarthy sprang out from his police vehicle. "What the fuck is this? He asked, surveying the scene. Several people approached him, all talking fast, and at the same time. "Shit, one at a time! He commanded. One of the people, a black lady, dressed in a high profile velvet pant suit, spoke up." I saw it ", she said, speaking with a faint southern accent. She continued, as McCarthy nodded. "The patrol car was moving fast, and hit the bus, rear ending it". McCarthy listened intently. "It appeared out of control", she finished, a look of horror on her face. McCarthy began taking peoples statements, verifying what the lady said. "Hey man", one youth said. He was about twenty, baseball cap lettered L.A. Dodgers, which was turned around on his head. "What? Asked McCarthy. Feeling very tired. The kid replied. "I saw a naked woman, thrown out of the cruiser". She got up and ran away. "Very sweet! He said, grinning. "Where? Asked McCarthy. The baseball cap guy pointed towards a dark alley. "Last time I saw her", the guy said. McCarthy stepped back to talk to a female officer, standing by. "What's your name? He asked her. "Patrol Officer Rose Calder", she stated, giving him a salute. "Never mind that" he said to her. "There's a naked woman running around loose, somewhere in that alley, he pointed. "I want you to check it out. "Could be dangerous, be careful". "Yes sir", she snapped, and took off down the alley. Taking her flashlight out, and placing her weapon underneath it. She slowly moved down the alley. Looking left, looking right, and up, her light brightened up the dark, and dank alley. Smells of old trash, urine, and vomit filled her nostrils. Christ, she thought, how disgusting! She shined her light on a stairwell to her left. The naked figure of a woman appeared in her light. Shocked, but still in control, Calder demanded, "Police, come down now! Alicia growled, and with acrobatic accuracy, bailed off the stairs, and collided with Calder. Calder caught by surprise, then her training kicked in. She struggled with the woman. Her pistol cocked, she fired three rounds at once. Into the woman's' head. Alicia collapse in a heap at Calder's' feet. Calder reached down to look at her. No doubt this bitch was dead. A shiver ran through Calder, as grey smoke erupted from the dead woman's mouth, into her nostrils, gagging her. She spun around, dropping her pistol. She vomited several times, and then straightens up. "I'm being invaded", was her last thought of her own. Smiling, now, she picked up her pistol, and holstered it. "Much better", she commented, then kicked Alicia's' body. "So long, bitch", she said to the dead body. Calder called on her shirt mike to McCarthy. "Calder here, subject is down, I repeat, subject is down. Grinning, she awaited for the other officers to arrive. "What happened? McCarthy asked, as he arrived." She jumped me! She exclaimed, just enough to make it her feel upset. She pointed at the dead girl; she shook a little, for extra affect. "Are you o.k.? He asked, lightly touching her shoulder. Calder shrugged, and then said, I'll be fine, just need a little time". McCarthy nodded, well . . . go back to the station there's probably going to be a shooting evaluation later". It's just routine, nothing to worry about". Calder turned away from him, and smiled. Now she could complete her mission, to finish Ben, at the hospital. Calder jumped into her squad car, an accelerated to the hospital.

Billy and Annie sat in the hospital room, waiting for their relief. Fifteen minutes later, still no arrival. Annie called dispatch. Annie turned to Billy. "The uniform is on the way". "They found Alicia'. "Where? Billy asked. Annie's face was pale. "She's been killed, after wrecking a patrol car and maybe killing the two officers inside". McCarthy is still at the scene, he wants us there, as we were the primary". The uniform officer Carl showed up at the hospitals doors. As he walked towards the doors, he saw a shadow in the bushes. He withdrew his pistol. "Come out, police officer! He commanded to the figure. A female uniform officer stepped out from behind the bushes. He recognized her, Rose Calder! A sweet thing, a rookie from the academy. "Damn! he said to her, "Scared the crap out of me! He holstered his pistol. "What the hell were you doing back there? Calder rubbed her hands together, like brushing something off. She stepped closer to Carl. "Had a call about a prowler, thought I'd look around." Carl nodded. "Got a babysitting job inside", he remarked frowning. Calder smiled, "Easy duty", she said. "Huh", he mumbled. Carl felt this was beneath him to do this, but orders are orders. "Find anything? He asked her. "False alarm", she said, stepping closer to him. She reached out to take his hand. Carl lifted his hand up, in a friendly gesture. Calder spun him around, grasping him in a choke hold. "What!" he, exclaimed. He struggled against her, while she dragged him into the brush. Carl was no light weight, at one hundred eighty pounds. He had sat his big butt to long in a squad car, and those garbage burritos had thickened his waist. Damn, she was strong for such a small woman. Carl felt his eyes rolling upward to the sky saying, adios! He furtively reached for his pistol, but couldn't reach it. He grappled weakly with her hands. He was becoming weaker by the moment. Then he felt his bowels unload. Hell of a way to die! He thought, as the darkness overcame him. He went limp, as Calder gave him a quick snap, breaking his neck. She dropped the body onto the ground. Brushing herself off, she sniffed at him. "How disgusting", she commented, stepping out of the bush. She checked her uniform over, and then breathed evenly. "Got to look professional", she cackled. Now to take of business the dark one had commanded. She stepped lively into the hospital, an approached the nurse at her desk, staring at a computer screen.

# Chapter Three

The nurse looked up at the female officer. The nurse, Rita by name, was from Haiti, and had come over to America ten years ago. She had hoped to find a better life for herself, and her two small children. She had scrubbed floors, cleaned toilets, and any other job she could get. Going to night school, she had completed her LVN training, and got hired right away. There was always a shortage for nurses in the area. She acknowledged the female officer. "Can I help you? She asked. "Room 1312, I've come to relieve the detectives", she stated in a flat, monotone voice. Rita pointed down the hallway, and gave Calder the directions. Thank you", replied Calder, still talking in a flat tone. Rita looked at Calder cautiously. Something about her, Rita thought. As she watched Calder going down the hallway, she had seen a brief vision of a dark aura around the officer. Then it disappeared! Rita shook her head. Must be fatigue from double shifts, she thought. Her mama had told her she had the gift of magic. Her father had been a voodoo priest. Rita had been instructed in the arts, but gave them up after going to the United States. She wanted to blend in with her new country. She had joined the Sacred Heart Catholic Church, and had attended mass when she could. She also joined the local PTA. Hoping if she kept busy, she would bury the magic into the dark recesses of her mind. Still, something bothered her about the female officer. Rita shrugged it off, probably just tired she thought. She went back to her computer screen. Calder entered the hospital room. "Are you our relief", Annie asked. "Officer Calder here", she intoned, nodding towards them. "Great! Billy said, "We have to go to a crime scene connected to our case, but we'll be back as soon as we can, he finished. "OK ", Calder said. Pointing at the bed, she asked, "Is that the child? "Yes", Annie replied, and then added, "There's been one attempt on his life already". Calder attempted a sympathetic face. "Poor baby", she said, "I'll take good care of him". Satisfied, Billy and Annie left to go to the crime scene. Calder looked around. No one here now, except Ben and his mom, and her. A fierce growl emitted from Calder's mouth. It was followed by a strong, foul odor of brimstone. She raced towards Bens' bed. She screamed at them. "You'll die you little bastard, and your bitch mom, too". Georgia screamed, attempting to stop her. They struggled briefly, sliding across the slick tile floor. Calder, fueled by black magic, was the stronger. She struck at Georgia's' head, flinging her against the wall next to the bed. There she hit the floor, unconscious. Calder turned towards Bens' bed. "Are you still in there, bitch? She roared at Ben. The Haitian nurse Rita scrambled into the room. Surprised, Calder turned towards Rita. "Get out cunt, or I'll kill you too" she yelled, in a low guttural voice. Rita stared in shock for a moment. Then she felt the power of voodoo coursing through her body, taking over. "Be gone evil one". Rita stated, staring at Calder, standing her ground. Calder distracted, advanced towards her. Rita spoke to her viciously. *"This is not how to be treat.* *"I'll shall not be bent".* *"I will use my hands and feet, and enemy shall be defeat!* Calder halted; a surprise of fear entered her face. At that moment, Rita struck her hard with a left hook. Then she kicked in Calder's' stomach. Calder bent, grunted, as if bowing. Rita gave her a final spinning kick to her face, which spun Calder against the hospital window. Calder reached out to gain her, and then fell through the window, shattering glass shards everywhere. She hit the ground with a sickening thud, as if deflating a helium balloon. Blood poured out in volumes on the smooth concrete ground. The slimy green smoke burst forth from her mouth, hesitating, then slowly dissipated. A doctor rushed in, his white lab coat flapping around him. Several nursing staff followed behind him. "What the hell is going on? He demanded, staring at the chaotic scene. "An attempted murder! Rita replied, catching her breath. Rita explained the situation to the doctor, leaving out the magic portion. She explained that she and the mom had struggled with the assailant and that she had accidentally fell out the window. The doctor quickly dialed the police dispatch. "Jesus! The dispatcher exclaimed, "It's been a crazy unusual day! The female dispatcher notified two police squad cars, and homicide detectives. The hospital staff heard police sirens not far away. Bens' mom was hugging him, and crying at the same time. The sirens roared through the night air making traffic move over to the side of the road.

# Chapter Four

The voodoo child woke up in darkness. Her hands and legs were bound to the walls by heavy metal chains. She strained against her bonds, to no avail. She was cast into the body of a drug addict. Her long blonde hair, straight, and flowing down her breasts, was observed by her. She was half naked, her t-shirt and bra gone, exposing her small, but firm breasts. How did she get trapped! By a mortal, no less! This mortal had bested her! Not in two thousand years had this happened. She looked down, seeing she just wore a pair of black panties, and nothing else. The panties were dirty, and her new found human sense of smell could catch the odor. Senses she never felt before assailed her! Mortals certainly are not very cleanly, she thought. The smells of her surroundings was new, and mysterious. The brief encounters into the human realm were short, and she concluded that it was best that way. She was ashamed. Trapped in this mortal body, she was all but helpless. The bokar had succeeded trapping her in the pentagram, and into a Govi jar. With the help of her nemesis, BACALOU, an evil spirit. She was ERZULE, goddess of wealth, protection, and vengeance. She felt not much of a goddess now, in this pitiful human form. There were track marks on her arms, from injecting drugs into them. The smell of her body odor offended her. She heard footsteps coming down the long winding stairs. The Bokar! She cringed, amazed now she felt human fear. She now knew his name. Arthur Sirocco! A practitioner of the black arts! Erzule grimaced in disgust as he approached her. She hung her head in shame. "Not feeling good today", he asked, smirking. She lifted her head, and gazed at him. He was of medium stature, and very thin. His once dark hair, thinning now, was turning grey at the edges. He wore a black robe, with a pentagram imprinted boldly on it. "Release me", she demanded, "And I'll let you die quick". Sirocco smiled. "Not today", he replied, "I have work for you to do". "I won't do your bidding anymore", she stated defiantly. "Oh, no", Sirocco said with an evil grin. He moved to her quickly. He slapped her face hard . . . once twice, with an open hand. The pain! The human pain! Her mind shrieked! "You'll do what I say, or else! Sirocco looked at her grimly. He began to remove his robe. He was naked underneath, his erection standing up obscenely at her. "No! No! She screamed. He reached over and ripped her panties off of her. Spreading her legs forcibly, he entered her. "Never fucked a goddess before", he grunted, thrusting into her. Screaming didn't help. It just excited him more. He climaxed with a shudder, and then drooled on her breasts. Erzule felt the human emotion of shame, and embarrassment. She had felt the involuntary reaction of an orgasm. Tears! Human tears rolled down her cheeks. Sirocco quickly put his robe back on. He tapped her cheek gently. Erzule held her head down, not screaming anymore. Sirocco grinned at her discomfort. "You be a good girl, and do as I say! He commanded. Naked, and hurting, Erzule nodded her head. Her eyes glowed a sharp reddish green. Sirocco continued over to a short metal table, where a Govi jar sat. Its inner self glowing bright yellow, illuminating the table. "Soon we will be together, again", he commented to the jar. The jar blinked several times, as if it understood. In it was the spirit of his dead wife, Melanie. She was Haitian, a very gentle soul. She had driven to the store to get groceries, when a drunk driver had t-boned her compact vehicle. He was in a ford f-150. The car tipped over an embankment, and the fuel tank of her car had been ruptured, causing it to catch fire. It exploded into a thousand pieces. Melanie's' body was thrown clear, a screaming ball of fire in the sky. Sirocco had felt something at that moment. A wave of nausea and dread overcame him. He dashed out to his humvee, and took off down the road. He came across the skid marks of a vehicle. He dashed to the edge of the embankment. In a look of stark horror, he saw the burning wreckage of his wife's' car. Nearby, he saw a charcoaled burning mass of flesh. It was his wife. "Oh, my god! He exclaimed climbing down to the mass of burnt flesh smoldering there. His face felt the heat emanating from the body. He halted, helpless, as the flame that destroyed his wife, simmered down. Wearing a light blue jacket, he attempted to cover his wife's body. As he bent and picked her up, a loud crack ensued, and she crumbled apart slowly in his hands. Sirocco sat down, and cried for a few minutes. Regaining his senses, he tried calling on his cell phone. No signal! He had to climb up the hill to get better reception. Slowly, he climbed the hill to make a call. He spied the ford truck, a hundred yards away, heavily damaged, but not burning. Sirocco clenched his fists, and moved hurriedly towards the vehicle. This was the one who took his wife's life! He peered into the trucks drivers' side. There was a man, possibly in his thirties, sitting there, blood streaming out his mouth, the steering wheel crushed against his chest. Sirocco could smell the rancid odor of alcohol, permeating the air in the truck. Several whisky bottles were scattered on the floor boards. "Help!" wheezed the man, his speech sounding like an accordion out of pitch. Siroccos mind began to bend, and snap. He grinned at the man. "You, betcha", he said, rubbing his hands together. "Be right back! Sirocco went to his humvee, and grabbed his spare one gallon gas can out. He returned to the truck. The man's left eye was swollen. He glanced with his good eye at him. "I got something here for you", Sirocco said. The man stared at him. Sirocco poured the contents of it all over the man. "NO! No, what the hell, he screamed at him. "I want you to feel what she did, you rotten bastard! Sirocco laughed, and then reaching for a match, he tossed it in the truck. The man lit up light a bonfire! Screaming and twisted, a crazy puppet on fire Sirocco laughed hysterically, then straightening up, he dialed 911. He relayed the information to the dispatcher, between sobs of grief. Standing there, almost in shock, he heard sirens in the distance. Police, ambulance, and fire department came flying up the hill. The police officer, a young rookie, approached the truck. Cracking the door open, the aroma of burnt flesh hit him; he turned and vomited on the ground. A paramedic looked in from behind him. "Crispy critter", he pronounced to himself. The fire chief approached Sirocco. He glanced down the hill, seeing the burnt mound of flesh. "How was that? He asked him. "My . . . my wife', Sirocco mumbled. His eyes rolled upward towards the sky, his knees buckled, and he collapsed into a heap on the ground. Sirocco came to in the hospital, still dazed. A nurse, who looked Haitian, resembled his wife a little. 'Mel . . ." he began, then closed his eyes. "How are you? She asked, "I'm your nurse, Rita". "My wife, my wife", he screamed at her. Rita produced a syringe, and quickly injected it into his left arm. "SSH", she said quietly, "You're going to be all right, honey". Sirocco relaxed, and then went into a deep sleep, no dreams pursued him. Rita gazed at the pitiful sight of the man. Somewhere, in the back of her mind, she felt a tingle of something ominous, dark. Shrugging it off, she left the room to continue her rounds of patients. Sirocco woke up the next day. He had been in and out of consciousness for twenty four hours. He had awaked thirsty, and hungry. Rita had brought a tray to him, with scrambled eggs, toast, bacon, and coffee. He consumed them greedily. Sirocco feeling better, left the next day. He developed a plan in his mind. Melanie had showed him some voodoo spells, and he planned on recovering her spirit. Leaving the hospital, he called a taxi. The driver pulled up, and Sirocco entered. The driver, who looked East Indian, turned to ask him, "Where to? "1207 Hospitality drive", Sirocco answered. Sirocco sat in silence the whole trip. They arrived ten minutes later. Sirocco paid the driver, and then exited. A sign colored in red, stood out from him. Magadenas Spell and charm Shop. As he entered, a bell rang, playing "Tubular Bells". Sirocco smiled, remembering the reference. A woman, Caucasian in looks, appeared from a back room. She was dressed in a red robe, with multi colored stars on it. She stood over six feet tall, and slender. Her hair was bright red. Like fire, and her breasts were marginally small for a very tall woman. "Can I help you? She asked, in a low voice sounding very masculine. Sirocco surprised, thought for a moment. Ah! A transgender, he thought to himself. Sirocco shrugged his shoulders. Whatever! He began explaining to her he wanted a Govi jar to recover his lost love. "Ok", he/she said in a masculine voice, going behind a dark black curtain in the back. Magadena returned with an oval, clear jar, the size of a jelly jar. "Forty dollars", Magadena said to him, handing him the jar. Without hesitation, Sirocco paid her. Magadena looked at him, puzzled. "For my deceased wife", he smiled at her. Something's wrong here, Magadena thought, but couldn't quite put her finger on it. She nodded his/her head, and then placed the money in the cash register. Magadena turned to face him, and gave a warning. "Be very careful, some floating spirits may try to gain entry when you do the transfer". Sirocco barely nodded, and then left, the bell ringing out its tune. Troubled by his/her feeling, Magadena returned to the back room, to consult her spell book, for some answers to the uneasy feeling that swept over her. Annie and Billy were almost to the crime scene. Billy was driving, when Annie's' phone rang.

She answered, a look of shock appeared on her face. "Oh, shit! She exclaimed. "What! Billy asked intent on his driving. "There's been another incident in Ben's room" "Goddamnit", Billy cursed, and swung a quick u turn in the middle of traffic. Horns blared through the air at him. Billy switched on his red light and siren, illuminating the despondent traffic. "Crazy night, huh? Annie asked him. Billy just nodded emphatically, his hands tightening on the steering wheel. They rushed through the night, wondering what the world has come to. Billy and Annie arrived at the hospital. They observed two squad cars, and the coroner's vehicle parked in front. The ambulance was parked nearby, no flashing lights were visible. Billy and Annie rushed in, drawing their firearms, just in case. A chaotic scene assailed their eyes. Ben's mom was crying, leaning over him. The nurse, Rita, was sitting on the floor, panting in exhaustion. A doctor, in his white lab coat, looked mortified. "What . . . ? Billy began. Annie helped the nurse to her feet. Annie looked at her quizzically. Rita shaken began to calm down, and then spoke. "It was evil . . . evil" she exclaimed. "What was it? Annie asked. Rita slowly explained the chain of events to her. Billy and the doctor listened, incredulously. Annie nodded her head politely, soaking up every word. "And that's it", Rita concluded, looking at Annie for a reply. Annie noticed the evil eye bracelet on Rita's right hand. Rita noticed her looking. "Are you a Mambo? Annie asked her quietly. Now I am", Rita stated proudly. She continued, "So are you". Annie developed a funny look on her face. "Huh? Annie asked her. Rita took Annie's right hand, squeezing it firmly. Annie almost jerked her hand back, on reflex. Rita looked into Annie's eyes. "You are a powerful one, but do not realize your great power yet". Rita released her hand, stating "My sister". Annie was speechless. Rita stepped away from her to check on her patient. Annie observed Rita whispering in Ben's ear. Ben's mom looked at her, and then smiled. "Protection for the child", Rita spoke softly. Annie's head was beginning to develop a small ache. Too much to chew on, she thought. Billy approached her. "What did he call you? He asked. "Mambo", Annie replied, looking him in the eye. She continued, "A powerful voodoo priestess". Billy grinned. "Are you", he asked. "No joke Billy. "My real parents were white and black magic and I think I inherited the skill". Billy's face looked grim. Then he spoke. "This voodoo stuff is hard to believe. But after tonight, I'm beginning to". Annie just shrugged her shoulders. The doctor was examining Ben, when he woke up with a start. "Mama! He cried out. Ben's mom broke down, tears cascading down her cheeks. "Oh, thank you, thank you", she murmured to Rita between sobs. Rita nodded solemnly. Annie looked at Billy. "We need to find the cause of all this". She continued, "Someone's' using black magic for some unknown purpose". "How? Billy asked. 'We can check with the local spells and charms shops", she replied. "There are two". One in Little Mountain and the other in town". Billy nodded, and replied, "First to other crime scene, before McCarthy chews out asses out." "A big order", Annie grinned. Billy smiled back at her. Annie turned to Rita. "Every thing good here? She asked. "Just fine "Rita replied, "Also two uniformed officers are stationed outside the room". "Good luck", Annie said to her. Annie and Billy left the room, the sounds of Ben's mom crying, and Rita chanting something in Haitian. Annie and Billy returned to the car, but first talked to the two officers, giving them instructions. They looked at Billy funny, but nodded in agreement, arriving at the scene; they saw Bud loading a body into his van, by two ambulance attendants. He turned to the two detectives. "Busy damn night", he quipped. "You got that right", Annie replied, approaching. Billy turned to Bud. "Overtime for you Bud? Billy asked, grinning. "Shit! Bud replied, "I'll be lucky if the county approves it". Bud turned away from Billy and cursed, "Cheap assholes! Bialy grinned at Bud's dismay. He got in with the ambulance. "Looks like Bud has a busy night", Billy commented to Annie. "Oh well", Annie said smiling. She continued, "It all pays the same". Billy grunted in acknowledgement. He started the car, and took off to the other crime scene. On arrival they saw McCarthy standing there, puffing on a cigarette, furiously, as if it would go out without help. "Hey boss", Billy hollered at him. "Shit! Shit! McCarthy said, pacing. McCarthy outlined the situation to them. Billy and Annie listened quietly to him. "Sounds like a connection to our case", Annie spoke. McCarthy listened to Billy and Annie's story of the hospital incident. "Voodoo, dodo", McCarthy said vehemently. He looked at Billy and Annie. "This crazy bullshit is all yours". Just fill me in on the results, and I'll try to square it with the top brass". With that, he stomped away to his car. Billy and Annie entered the alleyway. They walked carefully down it, and then spied a large cardboard box, covered in dirt and grime. It started to move! The pair unholstered their weapons, approaching it warily. A homeless man, dressed in tattered fatigues, emerged. His long hair standing out in strings of grease and dirt. The smell of body odor hung heavily in the air, like some dusky mist. Annie caught her breath, trying to ignore the smell. "Hey, don't shoot! ", the man said, grinning between his yellowed, rotting teeth. "What are you doing here? Billy demanded. "This is my home, I sleep here" the man said, pointing at the cardboard box. Billy and Annie looked at him curiously. "Did you see anything here? Annie asked, approaching him, carefully. "Hell yes, honey", the man replied, but I thought I was having the DT's". "Why's that? She asked, keeping her voice even. The man shrugged. "Got a butt? He asked. "Just a minute", Annie said. Stepping out of the alley, she saw a uniform puffing on his cigarette, looking bored. "Hey! She called to him. "What is it detective? He asked. She glanced at his name tag. "Officer Rinzulli", she said, reaching into his breast pocket to retrieve a cigarette, from his pack. "Hey! He said, starting to back up. "Give me your lighter, too", she demanded. He handed it over reluctantly. "Maybe by your own", he muttered, as she walked away. Annie ignored him, returning to the dark alleyway. "Here", she offered to the homeless man. The man took it, shaking slightly, and lit up, taking a few drags; He coughed several times, producing a slimy film, and then spat on the ground. Annie disgusted, pretended to ignore it. Then he spoke up, clearing his throat. "Ah, good", he said, and then continued. "I was trying to get some sleep, after finding half a bottle of wine, in the dumpster, "Annie nodded, encouraging him to continue." I saw the female officer enter the alley, and a crazy naked woman attacked her! He continued to puff on his cigarette. "The officer fired at the woman, and then she collapsed. Something bad, like green smoke, entered the officer, and then she became the crazy woman". "I could tell by the way her face looked, just like the crazy woman." He paused, then, finished up, "I could smell an odor, like trash burning for days". "How do you know? Billy asked, still doubting the man. "The smell! The man retorted. "I served in Desert Storm! "What happened? Annie asked politely. "Got lost somewhere", he replied, No help from the V.A.! He coughed again. He continued, "Started drinking, having flashbacks, lost everything and everybody". He reached inside his tattered filthy, fatigue shirt. He produced a shiny gold medal! The bronze star! This was no way for a hero to be. "There's a shelter just two miles from here". Go there! The man grunted, "Maybe". Annie went to talk to two uniform officers who had secured the crime scene. "There's a homeless man, a DESERT STORM hero, in there". One of the officers, Reed Winslow, looked at her intently. "I served then myself", he said. Annie said, "Take him to the nearest shelter. If he refuses, escort him there". "You got it ", he said, motioning to his partner to follow him into the alley. Despite the homeless mans protests, the two officers put him into the patrol car, and drove off. "Now what? Billy asked. "Let's go check those shops", "In the morning. My place is only three miles from here", Billy said. "Is that a suggestion? Annie said, smiling sweetly at him. Billy blushed, and then stuttered, "Uh, Uh, you can have the bed, and I'll take the couch." Annie laughed, as Billy's face turned a nice shade of red. "O.K. ", Annie said, nicely, wiggling her butt a little when getting into the car. "Oh boy", Billy mumbled to himself. Billy and Annie arrived at his one bedroom apartment. They climbed up the stairs to Billy's second floor apartment. Annie could here loud punk music next door. "Shit! Billy said. He walked over and beat on the door. He repeated several times. Then the door opened. A punker girl, her head shaved to one side, her hair a deep purple, and two nose rings, answered the door. "What's up, handsome", she smiled, smelling the sweet odor of pot on her. "Keep the noise down", He hollered over the noise to her. She grinned at him, staring at his crotch. Billy ignored her stare, and flashed his badge. "Turn it down, or get arrested! He said. The girl was smiling crookedly at him. "Oh! She cooed, holding out both of her tattooed arms. "I mean it, girl ", Billy said grimly. "Whatever you say five o ", she smiled again. As she turned to close the door, she lifted up her t-shirt, revealing her pear shaped firm breasts. Billy blushed. "I'm Pinky", she said, walking over to her stereo, and turning the volume down. "Let me know when you get lonely", she smiled again, closing the door between him. Amused, Annie looked at him. "Best offer this week? She asked, trying not to laugh. Billy mumbled something, probably not nice under his breath. Billy took out his key, and unlocked his door. "Come on in", he said to Annie, stepping aside to let her enter. Annie stepped in, gazing around the apartment. She observed several books on a bookcase. She walked over to look at them. Hmm! She thought. Several books on forensics and some mystery novels. The front room looked extremely tidy, for a bachelor. Everything in its proper order. She glanced into the kitchen. Everything clean and tidy. Pots and pans put away. The stove shined brightly, no grease visible. She looked in the cabinets. They were well stocked, and free of any dust. "Great! She mumbled, "My partner has OCD". Then she thought, maybe that's why he is so good at what he does! That way, he notices things missing or out of place at a crime scene.

Annie's gift was her basic instincts, feelings. Billy was what's missing! Annie shrugged. We complement each other, she thought. And any way, he has a cute butt! Annie grinned. Billy had gone into the bedroom, changing his clothes, from suit and tie, to blue jeans and a grey sweatshirt. Annie thought he still looked good. "I'll take the couch", Billy said, then went into the hall closet. He brought out a sheet and a blanket. He folded down the couch, which had a hide a bed in it. He properly made the bed up. Annie stood there amused. "The bedroom is all made up", he told her. He continued, Hope its o.k. "Annie smiled at him. "Oh!' she said sheepishly, I have nothing to change into". She went on, looking at him. "I guess I'll have to sleep naked". "Uh, o.k.", Billy said, finding it hard to swallow. Annie moved into the bedroom, turning with a grin on her face. "Night, Billy", she said, starting to remove her shirt. Billy grunted something, and then curled up in his blanket. The bed was made military style, old habits, Annie thought. Left over from the service! Annie stripped out from her clothes, and shoes. As she pulled her bra off, she gave a sigh of relief. It felt much better with the sisters out now. She snuggled up warm in the blankets. She fell asleep, dreaming of sex with Billy. She tossed and turned. Billy lay on the couch, half awake, thinking of Annie. God, she was beautiful! He felt lust swelling up. Then he heard soft footsteps, moving slowly towards him. "Oh, Billy", Annie's voice, gave out a moan. She stood in front of him, naked. He saw her perfect body, from her firm small breasts, to the dark revealing of mound of her pubic area. Her smooth long legs, athletic and just right, stood out. "Now, Billy", she said hoarsely, breathing quickly. Billy quickly took off his clothes, anxiously. He reached for her. She straddled his body, his hardness claiming to inside her. "I'm in command now" she gasped, moving her hips back and forth, thrusting. Billy moaned, his hands caressing her breasts. They moved in unison together. "Just right! She exclaimed, breathing hard, as she found her climax. Then Billy finished too. She bent down, kissing and hugging him. It felt good! Right or wrong as partners, they now felt certain intimacy in their lives. She took Billy's hand, and guided him into the bedroom. They consummated their bodies again. Exhausted, they fell asleep in each other's arms. Two hours later Billy's cell began ringing, again and again. "Aw shit! He mumbled, turning over burying his head in the pillow. Annie sat up. "Might be serious, she said scrambling out of bed to answer the cell phone next to an end table. "Hello", she said softly. A voice replied, "Annie? He asked, surprised. "Great, Annie thought, he knows were together now! It was McCarthy! "Just a minute", she said shyly. She reached over and nudged Billy with her elbow. "Billy", she urged, it's McCarthy". "Aw, fuck him", he said half awake. Annie nudged him again. "O.K., o.k. ", he mumbled, taking the phone. "Hey boss", he said, grinning at Annie, who got up to shower. She wiggled her butt at him. Billy grinned. "You better get down here", McCarthy growled. He continued, "We have another one", he said, 'In the orange groves, near Redlands. 'Shit! Billy said" We'll be there in thirty". "Having fun? Asked McCarthy. Billy knew the boss was smiling on the other end. Billy just grunted, and then hung up. Then he got into the shower with Annie. She laughed, while they played around for a few minutes, then dried out and got dressed. They descended down the stairs, and got into Billy's car. Billy hit the siren, red lights flashing in the daylight. "Annie looked at him. "Shit never stops, does it? Annie commented. Billy looked grim, and just nodded his head. They rushed off at high speed, heading for the orange groves. McCarthy had given those exact instructions how to get there. No way would they get lost! There were two sheriffs' cars, ambulance, and Bud Kline, the coroner. "Hail! Hail!" the gangs all here", Billy pronounced. Annie smiled at Billy. The two moved through the groves slowly. Lots of overgrown bushes lined the sides of the groves. The oranges were beginning to come out, displaying their rich glow of yellow in the warm sunlight. They saw Bud Kline leaning over a female body, brushing away the flies from it. McCarthy was standing behind Bud, trying to ignore the smell. He held a handkerchief to his nose, and pressed it there, while swatting at flies buzzing around. To the side of Bud, stood the ambulance crew. One female attendant turned pale, and vomited onto the bushes there. "Sorry", the male attendant said, "New girl". He produced a small vial of Noxzema, and handed it to her. "Put this in your nose, it will help ", he said sadly, remembering his first dead body he came to. "Thanks", she said, slightly embarrassed, checking to be sure she didn't get anything in her hair. Annie saw what was left of the female body. Her feet were lying carelessly to side of her. The legs themselves were missing! Her bloody torso and her head were all that remained. It was the once attractive head that got to them. Her eyes wide open, her mouth permanently open, as if screaming at the terror she was getting. 'Jesus", Billy said, his stomach churning a little. Then it settled down to a low rumble. Bud looked up, his face pale as a white washed fence, his mouth creased in a grim embrace. Annie leaned closer for inspection, her disgust over come by her professional observation. "Another Haitian woman", she commented. She continued, "By the appearance of the body, it was surgically cut, than cauterized, somehow". Bud confirmed her findings. He said "that's why there is very little blood". "Sadistic bastard", Billy said, "it looked like she was alive when it happened! Billy felt concern for Annie. She was Haitian! He knew Annie could take care of herself, but he would still worry about her. Annie looked over the body, carefully. The girl was possibly only eighteen years old! Too young to die! What was this perp doing? Stealing body parts! Was it for trophies? Or was he some kind of fucked up Doctor Frankenstein?

# Chapter Five

The attendants loaded up what was left of the victim. Bud Cline said, "Meet me at the morgue, I have something to show you, and tell you! Bud looked ashen, and shaken. Very unusual behavior for him. Behavior for him. "O.K. ", Billy said, looking at Bud questionably. McCarthy stated, "the press gets a hold of this, everything will turn to crap'. He continued, "Shit rolls downhill". Annie replied, "That's what they pay you the big bucks for boss". "McCarthy commented, "Not enough, you should see my alimony payments". He then turned in a huff, and left in his car. Annie and Billy left, driving towards the morgue. Billy commented, along the way, "Bud acted pretty sketchy'. Annie turned to look at him, "More than usual! The two arrived at the morgue, after dodging afternoon traffic. The morgue was a stark pale white color, where it stood out among the more colorful businesses. Only one story, it looked sadly out to the street. The grave monument to its serious business in side. Annie and Billy strode into the basement where the morgue resided. They walked slowly down the stairs. Entering the morgue door, they observed Bud, pacing, sweat pouring from his brow, cascading down to his shirt. His bald head shimmered with perspirations. "What's so important? Annie asked. Several bodies lay on the cold steel tables, some covered up, and some exposing their torsos. The one from the first crime scene lay exposed to them. Bud looked excited, and disturbed. 'Here! He announced, exposing her mutilated body. "What! Asked Billy, irritated that he couldn't see anything. Nothing unusual! Bud stammered, "It . . . It spoke to me". Bud started shaking. "Huh? Annie asked. Has Bud flipped out, she pondered. Bud stammered again. "It . . . it said, help me Maga". He continued, 'then a puff of yellow smoke erupted from her mouth". "I sweat I heard a scream, then the smoke evaporated". Annie thought, any minute now he was going to collapse from nervous exhaustion. "Bullshit", Billy exclaimed, sounding doubtful, but still unsure of it. Annie approached him, "Calm down", she said reassuring him. She asked, "Been drinking lately? Annie knew Bud had gone through a bad time with his divorce of his wife, Julie, a temperamental redhead. Bud just shook his head, no. He went on, "I'm going home early, and get well saturated there". Annie and Billy left, Billy shaking his head in disbelief. As they started to get in the car, they saw Bud coming out, mumbling to himself. "I'll let my assistant finish up in autopsy". Bud got into his maroon Ford Expedition, and took off. Bud lived out near Victorville, in the boonies. Bud travelled down the freeway, till he got to his exit, and turned off to an unpaved dirt road. He could hear the dirt rattling along his tires. Then an ominous smell assailed his nose. It smelled like . . . brimstone, collecting itself around and in the truck. "What the fuck! He said startled. Looking ahead, he could see green, slimy looking smoke gather upon the hood of the truck. It swirled around it, like some crazy dust devil. It slowly began taking shape! The shape, becoming fully formed, was visible to Bud. The figure appeared in a black shining robe. The grinning face of a skull leering out at him. Bud screamed, swerving the truck back and forth, trying to shake the evil vision off the truck! A scythe, long and sharp appeared in its skeletal arms. The specter swung the implement in a wide arc, crashing down on the hood, making a loud crunch, and tearing at the metal. The flash of metal, as if it was burning, assailed Bud's nose. Bud kept swerving back and forth again, trying to shake it. Bud screamed again "You sonofabitch! More burning metal flew from the truck. Bud could see the scythe flaming hot, strike his hood again! The truck spun around, as if making a crazy u-turn, and then went flying into the ditch, the tires screaming out in hopeless agony. Bud heard a gravelly voice that pierced his brain, like a sharp blade inserted there. It said, "Warning, back off! Then the shape dissipated into the air, as if it was never there. Bud sat there shaking. Sitting down, he looked at his trousers, which was heavily soiled. Then he passed out.

Annie and Billy decided to get something to eat, they went into Sanbernardino, and stopped at a Denny's. They sat down, then ordered something off the menu, and then ordered coffee. The waitress returned with their drinks. Billy looked out the window to the mini mall there. Annie glanced over, sipping her coffee. "Hey! Billy exclaimed "We're next to a mini mall". Annie replied, pointing towards a row of shops a sign in one of the shops windows read: MAGADENA's Charm and Magic SHOP. Open seven days a week, 10 A.M. to 8pm. Billy and Annie ate their lunch quickly. They strolled over to the shop. A sign was pasted in the window, declaring it open. Annie opened the door, and the door chimes rang clearly, with a tone from Tubular Bells. "Tubular Bells", Annie commented, smiling. Billy looked at her puzzled. 'It's from the Exorcist movie" she explained. Billy nodded. They looked about the shop. Rows of wooden shelves held various herbs, spices, and charms were positioned there. Inside a glass, Annie noticed a withered hand, its palm facing upward, as if complaining its' current situation. The hand of glory, Annie thought, and then shivered, used in some spells. Billy looked at it, with a disgusted, bored look on his face. A figure appeared from behind a velvet curtain towards the back of the room. He, she looked at them. All the appearance of a female but not. The man/woman was very tall, at least six feet. His / she were dressed in a red robe that matched the long curly red hair cascading down the shoulders. "Can I help you? Magadena asked, in a low, soft voice. Magadena continued, "Have I done something? "Madam", Billy said hesitantly, just a few questions". "You have badges officers? He /she moving up to the counter 'Anything for you, cutie", He/she grinned at him. Annie grinned at Billy's `discomfort. "Pre or post op? Annie asked Magadena. "Pre", sighed Magadena, sighing. "You are? Annie asked him/her politely. "Magadena", the redhead replied, this is my shop". Annie thought, Magadena . . . Maga, Maga, the name she recalled from before. The voice of the dead woman pleading for help! "We have two bodies in the morgue both Haitian girls". She continued, watching for the redhead's reaction. Annie continued, 'One of them after death, called out your name". "Oh, no! Magadena said, grasping the edges of the counter. "Do you think you might know them asked Annie. "Maybe a part of your circle? Magadena gasped, "My assistant Juby, did not come to work today" "Can you close up shop, and then come with us? Annie asked, showing some empathy on her face. "Maybe you can identify them! 'Evil is everywhere! Magadena declared, shivering. Magadena then said to Annie, "May I see your hands? Annie shrugged, and held her hands out, palms up. Magadena grasped her hands firmly, and closed his/ her eyes. mumbling some incantation in Haitian language. Magadena shivered, and Annie began doing so too. Billy tensed up, stepping forward to intervene. A deep male voice growled at hi. "Don't", it warned, your woman is all right! The voice continued, "We are communicating! Billy stopped, stood still, waiting nervously. Annie's eyes rolled upward, only the whites showing, like two egg whites in a pan. Magedena's body slowed down, as Annie's body did the same. They both relaxed, as Magadena released her hands. Annie stood, her knees feeling weak, shaking her head like recovering from a blow to the head. 'What . . . What was that?, Annie stammered. Billy moved forward angrily, his fists clenched. "What the fuck did you do to her? He demanded. "Nothing", Magadena smiled, "Just getting in touch with her ancestors, and the great power, she possess. Annie smiled at him, trying to placate him. "Its o.k.", she said weakly. "The hell is going on! He demanded to her. Magadena shrugged slightly, looking apologetic. "She a descendant of Papa Legba, a great voodoo man". She continued further, "it's been passed down the generations to her". 'Her parents were witch, and warlock, and were murdered by a jealous rival". Annie gave Billy a shy smile. 'I think I know that now", Billy said in amazement, not sure still what was going on, but glad Annie was all right. He unclenched his fists, relaxing his body some. 'I'll close up shop, and go with you', Magadena said, grabbing the keys off the counter. Magadena came out to them from behind the counter. Damn, Billy thought, that's one big man? Or woman! Magadena smiled at him, noticing he was looking. "Interested, curious? The he/she asked, sexily. Billy blushed. "No, thank you", he said, trying to be polite. 'you should keep this one", Magadena said, winking at Annie. "I have something for you1, Magadena said to Annie. Returning back to the counter, she produced a shiny silver bracelet, garnished with various types of charms on it. "This would make him your sex slave, honey; Magadena chuckled, handing the bracelet to her. Billy's face burned red. Annie laughed, than placed it in her jeans pocket. "Great! Billy mumbled. The trio left to get into Bill's car. "I'm shorter, so I'll get in back", Annie said, with a straight face. Billy mumbled something the other two couldn't hear. Magadena slid inside the passenger's seat, smiling. She leaned over to Billy. "I don't bite . . . much. She laughed. Billy mumbled something, and then started the car. "Put on your seatbelt ", he said tersely. He drove off. Sirocco gazed down on his handy work. A pair of feet and legs was spread upon the steel table. He placed them together, and then began chanting in Haitian, The feet and legs began slowly growing together, with a slushy sound as they connected, sinew and bone. The parts were now assembled seamlessly. The voodoo child looked on, rattling her chains. Disgusting! She thought. If only I could get free! She could destroy the man, and his abomination! Then she could be restored to herb former self. She had been forced to send an evil spirit to terrorize someone. She felt helpless. "You will pay for your evil indiscretions", she shouted at him. Sirocco turned, grinning at her. "Don't think so", he quipped. Then he continued, "I can't free you, I see the hate and loathing on your face". He kept going, "you will be my slave, as long as I live! "I hope it's a short life mortal", she retorted to him. Sirocco turned his back on her. As long as he kept her bound in chains, with the slave necklace around her neck, she could do nothing. She could only wait for the right moment for her bid for freedom. Then she would tear him apart, all the way down to his very soul! Then she would scatter what was left into the darkness! Her nemesis, Bacalou, had taken over some of the mortal's soul already. The darkness would grow inside the man, Sirocco was unaware. Soon it would consume him. Voodoo child lapsed into serious thought, and then fell asleep, dreaming of being whole again. Somewhere in the background, she heard Bacalou laugh! Annie and Billy, with Magadena arrived at the morgue. A nervous Johnny Dugan, assistant coroner, stood at the steel tables, where the bodies lay. "Glad you're hear", he said, rubbing at his forehead. "What's the deal? Annie asked Johnny. Dugan frowned. "Bud called me", he replied. He continued his normally grim face pale, like a sheet of notebook paper. "Bud called . . . he said, something attacked him on the road! "He wasn't making much since, sounds like he had been drinking! "So", Billy commented. Dugan replied, "I've never seen or heard of Bud being intoxicated". "He rarely drinks. Maybe one or two beers". Annie just shook her head. She then asked, "What about them? As she pointed to the bodies. Dugan looked nervously, nodded his head back and forth. "I swear to God the female on the other table sat up, and screamed, "My legs! Then she lay back down. "A puff of yellow smoke burst forth from her! Dugan turned away from the bodies, staring wildly, looking at the three. Magadena stepped forward, lifting the sheet of the legless woman. "Damn! He/she exclaimed, it's Juanette, a powerful mambo! She leaned close to her, and then pulled her mouth open. "Her soul has moved on", Magadena commented, with a sigh. She did the same thing to the first body, which was missing her feet. "So has she! Magadena exclaimed. Magadena continued, "There is terrible black evil coming, and we can't stop it! He/she covered the body back up with the sheet. She mumbled something Haitian over the two bodies. The bright lights and smell of disinfectant assailed her senses. Magadena stood straight, as if at attention. His/her eyes rolled up, the whites only showing. Then Magadena collapsed slowly onto the floor. She began to shake, and mumbling in some strange tongue! "Oh shit! Billy exclaimed, "She's having a seizure! "I don't think so", Annie stated, leaning over Magedena's prone body. Annie leaned close to him/her, to hear well. "Communicate, Laveau'. Laveau, Hurry, Hurry! The voice was not Magedena's, but a female with a slight French /Haitian accent!*VouisAiderA!*, The voice finally pronounced. Annie glanced at Billy. Both he and Dugan stared in amazement. "What.. What was that! Billy stammered. "Contact with another spirit", Annie answered him. "WH . . . What? Asked Dugan mumbling. 'Never mind", Annie told him, attempting to wake Magadena up. Annie shook the unconscious body, several times. Magadena opened his/her eyes, and then blinked at Annie. "What happened? Magadena asked, slowly rising from the floor. "A contact from beyond", Annie replied to Magadena assisted him/her up. "Who? Magadena asked. 'I believe it was Marie Laveau", Annie replied. "I think? Magadena said, "Oh my! "We must contact her! Then Magadena asked, "What did she say? Annie looked at him/her. "Help you, she said in French. Magadena straightened up. "We must have a séance to reach her". "This is to fucking weird for me", Dugan said, then left the room. Magadena watched him leave. "Touchy guy", Magadena said smiling. Magadena continued, "Tonight at midnight, we need to reach h her before it's too late. Annie nodded, and Billy protesting, finally agreed. They dropped Magadena off at her shop, and headed for the office. Feeling tired, they entered the sheriffs' station. Several detectives and uniformed deputies sat at their desks, either typing typing up their reports, or scanning their computer screens. The computer tech, Marlon, greeted them, while frowning over something on the desktop screen. McCarthy appeared; looking harassed lo, his hair a mess, his tie hanging loosely around his neck. "About time", he said, I've got the mayor and chief of Ds chewing on my butt over this! "We have some leads", Annie stated. Billy retorted, "That's why we're here, to finish our report". McCarthy grunted, and turned to Marlon. He smiled at him. "I got some hate mail for you to check,

Marlon." He continued, "It says, cops stick it up your ass". He handed Marlon the mail. He handed the mail to Marlon. Marlon replied, "Thanks, but I'm a little sore from last night". He continued, "Is that an offer? He asked, grinning. McCarthy's face turned red, mumbled something unintelligible, and stalked off to his office. Annie and Billy laughed. They new Marlon was gay. Several detectives at their desks guffawed. McCarthy opened his office door, and said angrily, "You people have something better to do! Everyone at their desks bent over the computers, acting busy. McCarthy slammed his office door with a bang, shaking it. Annie and Billy sat down at their desks, composing each other's versions of the report. They compared the reports, and satisfied, Annie knocked on McCarthy's' door. "What! Yelled McCarthy through the door. "Our reports", Annie said bravely, stepping into the office, with Billy trailing behind her. The pair handed him their reports, waiting for the bomb to fall. The reports were at least three pages long, and very detailed. McCarthy frowned, and then reached into his breast pocket for his glasses. The pair looked at him. Putting them on, he said, "They're just for reading". "And writing". McCarthy scanned the reports, frowning further. "Damn! He exclaimed, glancing at the two. "I'll have to clean this up for the chief to look at". Billy stated, "That's an understatement! McCarthy sighed, "Following your lead up later? The pair nodded at him, turned about, and left. McCarthy shook his head. How the hell was he going to present this crazy crap to the chief? Annie and Billy, trying to stay awake, finally made it to Billy's apartment. They both entered, and collapsed on the bed, fully clothed, fell asleep in each other's arms, and no dreams haunted them.

# Chapter Six

Armand Jeneta sat at his desk, drumming his fingers on it, staring into space. His daughter, Angelica, had run away two months ago. Being the Inland Empire's major crime boss, he felt helpless trying to find his daughter. She had run away the night he had his brother murdered, Tony. Armano had risen up in the ranks of crime. First as an enforcer, then a right hand man to his boss, Giuseppe Montego. The old boss was to set in his ways, refusing to expand into the drug trade. Armano had married the boss's daughter, Monica. But he was greedy, and

And ambitious, and he and his brother Tony, plotted to get rid, of the old boss. So one night, they waited for the old guy to come out of his favorite restaurant, Antonio's. Armano and Tony hid behind abandoned, beat-up old ford pickup. They saw the boss and his bodyguard, Tiny, come out. Now Tiny was a misnomer for him. He stood six foot five, and weighed in at three hundred pounds. But the soft living he had as a body guard, had slowed his reflexes gradually. The two assassins had counted on this! As Tiny opened the door for his boss, the two sprang into action! Stepping out from behind the Junker, they aimed their ar-15 at the target. Tiny saw them, surprised, but pulled his .357 magnum out. Too slow! Tiny was hit by a volley of bullets. Still he fell over, trying to protect his boss. The two ambushers ran forward, still firing. Bullets erupted through the Buick of the bosses' car. Tiny jerked spasmodically, as the gunfire increased. Armano stepped up cautiously, to the two bodies lying in the street. He heard a noise coming from underneath Tiny,s body. The boss was alive still, but bleeding out copiously. Armano leaned over to him. "Sorry boss", He said softly, just business". With that, he emptied the rest of his clip into the bosses' face, obliterating it completely. "It's done",. He said to tony, let's go! With that they took off, as the sirens of the police grew nearer. Armano reached home, changing clothes, and approached the stairs leading to bedroom. He held a grim face as he approached his wife, lying in bed, due soon to give birth. "I have some bad news, honey", he said attempting to put on a sad face. Monica, a beautiful but very pregnant blonde, sat up in bed, her eyes focusing on him. 'What . . . what is it? she asked in a timid, but fearful voice. "It's your father, he was ambushed with Tiny, and they both were killed! "Oh my god", she said. Then she glared at him, her eyes showing anger and hate. "You . . . You bastard! She screamed, "I know you did it you creepy bastard! "Calm down", he replied to her, "The baby". "Fuck it, I'm leaving, ", she retorted, getting out of bed, dressed only in a shimmering white nightgown. 'Oh shit! She yelled. Looki8ng down, her water had broken! "Damn! He said, looking down. "I'll call the ambulance". Monica screamed obscenities at him, as he dialed. The ambulance arrived, rushing her to the hospital. As they wheeled her into the delivery room, she screamed at him. "Murderer, murderer, my baby's daddy is a monster! The attendants and doctor looked at him. "She's hysterical", Armano said, putting an expression of sympathy on his face. The attendants and doctor nodded empathy to him. They wheeled her into the labor room, where she kept up screaming. Then all was still. The doctor stepped out, an hour later, to confront Armano. 'Do you know what she was upset about? "No, haven't a clue", Armano replied. "I have good news, and bad news", the doctor told him grimly. "What is it? Armano asked, dread in his voice. "Complications of an early delivery, doctor said, resign in his voice. "Tell me! Armano demanded. "You can only save one of them", the doctor stated frankly, keeping his voice even. He continued, "Your wife, or the baby! Armano gasped, feeling like he was in some kind of horrible dream. "I need to know now, to save one", the doctor concluded. "Uh . . . uh", Armano stuttered. Then thought, the . . . the baby! "All right! The doctor said, returning returning to the labor room. A half hour later, the doctor returned. "It's a girl", he told him. Armano half smiled then collapsed on the floor. The night's events caught up to him. Armano sat in deep thought at his desk, the sweet and bitter of it all. Now he had to deal with his brother Tony! The word was Tony was conspiring to eliminate him, and take over the business. Armano believed this. He and Tony were cut from the same cloth, both greedy and ambitious. Disloyalty, especially from family could not be tolerated. With a heavy burden of reluctance, he called Tony for a meeting. Armano waited patiently. The doorbell rang. "Come in", Armano shouted, cheerfully. Armano new that Tony would would bring his two bodyguards. So he had his right hand man, Johnny Burkowski, hide on the staircase, behind a row of roses, in a flower pot next to the spiraling staircase. Johnny was Polish, a big bruiser at six eight, and three hundred pounds, His dark hair slicked back, and his gun metal eyes revealed no emotion in them. Armano was short, and slim, weighing about a buck fifty. Johnny towered over him. Armano though, felt safe and secure around him. Johnny had been his body guard for ten years now. His imposing frame, kept others at a distance. A faithful soldier Johnny had been! Tony stood at in front of Armano's desk, his two body guards flanking him to the left and right. "What's up? Asked Tony politely. Armano smiled at him, looking at the open drawer of his desk, revealing a .357 magnum. "I've heard some disturbing rumors about you, Armano stated flatly, looking his brother straight in the eye. "Well rumors are just bullshit gossip, bro, Tony said, fidgeting a little. Tony shifted his weight, spreading his feet apart, beginning to tense up. Sweat began to form on Tony's brow, his eyes growing larger. "Well now, the man who told me was very reliable", Armano stated, keeping his poker face. Armano reached under his desk, and tossed Tony a medium six box. Tony stepped back from the box. The box rolled up at Tony's feet. A head rolled out, revealing its horrible grimace, in death! "Shit! Tony swore. "Recognize him, Armano grinned evilly. It was there cousin, Alfredo! Armano glared at his brother. "He talked quite a bit for I killed him! Tony reached for his gun, inside his jacket. But the gun got hung up in his shoulder holster. He scrambled clumsily with it. Armano quickly drew his magnum from the drawer. He fired at Tony, blowing a big hole into his face, scattering brains and blood on his two body guards. In shock for a moment, the man on the left withdrew his gun. This was Johnny's chance! He fired several rounds at the man, hitting him in the back of the head, splattering brain matter all over the right man's jacket. Cursing, the man spun towards Johnny, trying to level his pistol. Johnny was faster. He fired three more shots. The target was hit all three times, once in the man's shoulder, one in the chest, and another in the groin. The man stood, staring in disbelief, at his wounds, and then collapsed in a heap on the floor. Armano came out from behind his desk, and kicked the lifeless body of his brother. "You sonofabitch Why! "We were blood! He heard a gasp, then a female screaming. It was his daughter, Angelica! She stood at the top of the stairs, and then shaking, she vomited. Looking down on the carnage, she ran back to her room to her room, slamming the door. "Oh, damn", Johnny lamented, putting his gun away. Armano paled, seeing her. "Go get her, Johnny ". Johnny made it up the stairs in three strides. Armano shook his head. Tony was her favorite uncle. Johnny banged on the girls door. "Go the fuck away", she yelled at him from behind the door. "Come on out, honey", Johnny said smoothly, trying the lock. It wasn't about to open, she had locked the door tight. Johnny knew better than to try and break it in. Johnny yelled down at Armano. "Want me to break it? "No! No! ", Armano yelled back to him, "Just let her be! Armano continued, "I'll talk to her when she has calmed down". Armano shaken, turned to his liquor cabinet to make himself a drink. Damn!, he thought, how am I going to square this with my daughter! Several of Armano's crew showed up from next door, having heard the shots. "What do you want done, boss? Johnny asked, coming down the stairs. Armano gazed down on the bodies. "Take them to the meat shop, grind them up for kibble, and scatter them in different locations at the lake". Johnny nodded, instructing several men to wrap the bodies in plastic bags, and carry them out where a black van was parked in front. The crew drove off with the bodies, while Johnny remained by his bosses' side. Angelica sat in despair in her room, brooding. She began crying again. She had known by the age of eight, her father was a gangster. But he always had been gentle to her, and kept his crime life from her. Tonight was the shock of her life. Angelica was tough in her own way, much like her father. She stripped off her pale blue nightgown, and slipped into her blue jeans, and a black tank top. Her father had killed her favorite uncle, and two of his men. Tony with his easy grin, had brought her presents, when she was young, than later gift certificates for various shops. Angelica decided to run away. She had a boyfriend Largo, now for three weeks. Largo was in his twenties, a handsome Puerto Rican, short at five seven, and only one hundred thirty pounds. His dark hair was cut short. He was a drug dealer of Heroin, and Cocaine. Angelica had known most criminal types since childhood, so Largo's profession didn't bother her. He was always kind to her, and lavished her with small gifts, and admiration. She climbed out the bedroom window, skimming down slowly on the large oak door outside her window, hitting the ground softly. She looked about, no one outside now! She turned to look at the modern two story brick house she grew up in. "Fuck all of you! She said angrily, and then rushed out through the woods, heading for town. She was going to hook up with Largo, and get way from all this shit! She reached into her jeans pocket, and produced a cell phone, and called him. "O.K. baby", he said softly, I'll come to the edge of town to pick you up". Angelica hurried through the woods, brushing aside the low hanging branches there, excitedly, to meet her lover. They had sex twice, snorting a small amount of Cocaine. She loved the feeling it gave her. Free, and uninhibited. Her orgasmic level went through the roof. It was the greatest thrill she ever experienced. Looking forward to more, she reminisced while she walked, the glaze of happiness in her eyes, glowing. Largo picked her up in his 1972 beige Monte Carlo. A beautiful classic! She had loved this car right from the beginning. She scooted closer to him, putting her hand on his thigh. He was getting hard! She could feel it through his pants. Largo wore a silk shirt, with brown khakis. They had made love in the back seat several times before. He breathed heavily. He gave Angelica a look. "Let's get into the back seat". I'm going to pullover". Excited, they jumped into the back seat, taking their clothes off. They had sex quick, climaxing together, in a rush of heat. A car zoomed by, full of teenagers. One leaned out the window and yelled, "Wow! I'm impressed! Angelica gave him the finger, and Largo laughed. They quickly got dressed, and headed for town. Several weeks later, their relations got bad to worse. Largo had introduced her to a new buddy! Black tar Heroin! She was hesitant at first, and then when he injected her, she felt amazing! Her daydreams were filled with romantic interludes with Largo. Largo smirked at her. She was almost ready. He had someone interested in fourteen year old pussy. Jumbo, a three hundred black pimp, was coming over. He owed Jumbo a favor he had bailed Largo out on some drug charges. Jumbo also had fronted him a large amount of Heroin, for sale. He was going to give Angelica to him, to pay Jumbo back. She wasn't going to go peacefully, so he had a plan to force her. She was just a commodity, like Heroin. Her helpless dreams of love would be shattered. Largo called to her to come in the front room. Angelica looked bored, setting her romance magazine down on the leather couch. "Let's get high", he said, producing a syringe, already loaded. She smiled at him. "Sex after? She asked, smiling. 'Hell yes! He said. He hoped his timing would be good, on getting rid of her lazy ass! After she reclined on the couch, nodding off, he called Jumbo. Angelica slipped into a daydream, her eyes fluttering. Dreaming of her wedding to Largo. She walked down the aisle, alone. Largo stood in front of the priest. The priest was Father o' Brian. From her church in her childhood. He smiled at her. She looked down at her wedding gown. A Baby blue floor length dress. She hefted it a little, from dragging the floor. But who was giving her away. As she stood at the pulpit next to Largo. The priest intoned, "Who gives the bride away? She heard a pitter patter of feet, made louder by what was probably three inch heels. She turned her head slightly around to see who it was. It was her mother! Largo gripped the girl's hand tight, almost squeezing it. Her mother, who she never met, looking picture perfect in a beige, flowing gown, raced towards the two. "Mama! Angelica cried. "Stop! Stop It! her mother screamed, her high heels clacking along the tile floor, like horses hooves. "What! Cried out Angelica. Largo held her right hand in a sturdy grip, almost crushing it. The priest began his ceremonial incantation. It was the last rites! "Do you confess your sins to the almighty", He bellowed out. Angelica stared at the priest. He began shifting in shape, his flesh slowly creeping apart. Angelica screamed, turned to Largo. Largos flesh began away too, revealing a half eaten corpse, maggots protruding from his eyes. He turned to her. "Give me a kiss baby! "Your mine now! He cackled as more slimy maggots began squirming their way out his mouth. Angelica screamed! She looked up at the priest, now just bones rattling. He extended one bony arm, "Ashes to ashes, dust to dust'. The skull grinned at her, and then the bones hit the floor in a loud clatter. Angelica kept screaming, trying to pry her hand from Largo, his corpse face grinning at her. Her mother approached the two, and pushed and pulled Largo away from her, his arm, still clinging to her. Her mother started slapping her face, harder and harder. "Why, Mama? She asked her mother, tears running down her cheeks. "Wake up baby", her mother said, "You're in danger, Wake up! Angelica squirmed in her sleep. She awoke, feeling a sting on her wet cheeks, crying. Jumbo, only a mile away, showed up at the door. Largo answered it. There stood a huge black man, Heavy set, taller as large as he was fat. "Is she ready? He asked. She will be", replied Largo, pointing to her, sitting on the couch, dazed. Jumbo stepped over to her, and slapped her face twice. "Snap out of it baby, time to put your ass to work". 'Fuck you! Fuck you! she screamed in his face. She felt something being attached to her wrists. Plastic zip ties! Binding her fast. "Time to go baby", Largo smirked at her. She screamed at him, trying to kick him. Largo just laughed at her futile attempt. "Time to get another one, someone fresh". "You're damaged goods ", he laughed. Jumbo pulled her up straight, her tiptoes barely touching the floor. He dragged her out, in only her cotton panties. He then tossed her bodily into his Mercedes back seat. She continued screaming and kicking. Jumbo laughed, then drove off to what he calls his pimp pad. As they arrived, jumbo grinning, yanked her out of the car, and half carried her to his house. She was crying hysterically. Jumbo ignored her. Pulling her into the house, she sagged a little from exhaustion. A light skinned black girl stood Maggie, Jumbo's number one girl. "Got a new face for you Mags", he said. Maggie looked her over. She towered above the girl at five foot nine, and one hundred forty pounds. Her eyes stared sadly at Angelica. Poor thing! She thought, Being stuck in this kind of life, and so young! Jumbo pushed the girl, closer to Maggie. 'Clean her up, Mags, "he said then continued, "Dress her up in something sexy". Maggie just nodded; defying Jumbo was a bad idea! She had felt his anger before! Not leaving marks on her face, he had pummeled her breasts and stomach before. Maggie sighed, taking the plastic ties, off Angelica's hands. "She'll be o.k. ', she said to Jumbo, escorting the girl to the bathroom. She whispered in Angelica's ear. "Go along with it, or you'll get hurt". Angelica dazed looked at her. "I know what it's like" She raised her blue silk blouse, showing purplish marks on her stomach, beginning to fade away. Angelica stared in horror. "We girls got to stick together, honey", Maggie said softly. Maggie helped her out of her panties, giving the girl and admiring look. She smiled. "Sorry", she said, "I do prefer girls, but not against their will! Angelica stepped into the shower, and ran the warm water down her body. The blast of the water, made her feel much better! She cleaned herself up, scrubbing vigorously. Getting out she dried herself off. Maggie had left, returning with a purple tank top, and a white mini-skirt. No panties, no bra! Maggie smiled, 'Yes, he likes it that way, no bra and no panties, when you're on the stroll! Angelica looked at her puzzled. "That's right honey, we are prostitutes". Angelica slipped on her top and min-skirt, noticing her light pubic hair was barely covered. Angelica shrugged, thinking this is my life for now, get over it bitch! Maggie was going to show her the ropes of being a hooker. Angelica listened carefully to Maggie's instructions. "Money up front or those cheap bastards will take off without paying". The best way is to offer them head, it's quick and you can move on to the next john. Twenty five for head, and no vaginal or anal sex." It's bad enough we have to swallow it". Angelica listened. Maggie was her only friend now, and she hoped she would help her get away some day. The pair hit the streets, looking for johns. Many middle aged men preferred Angelica. She was young and pretty, and hadn't developed the burned out look, the older ones had. Maggie steered the more rough ones her way, protecting the girl. After three weeks, Angelica began tiring of giving ten blowjobs a day. Maggie saw it in the girl's eyes. She decided on a diversion to lift Angelica's spirits. Maggie took her to a friend of hers, Magadena, who owned a voodoo shop. Magadena, a transgender greeted them heartily, looking sadly at Angelica. "This girl doesn't belong on the streets", Magadena said, angrily. Magadena gave Angelica an evil eye bracelet, for her protection. "This should keep you safe", said Magadena, chanting some alien words upon the girl. Magadena stared into the girl's eyes, a look of consternation flowed on her face. Angelica, fascinated, just nodded. Smiling, she thought, at least now I have two good friends! "Come here, mama", Magadena said to Maggie. Maggie, happiness on her face, stepped forward. She took Maggie's hands, and closing her eyes, mumbled something to Maggie, Angelica couldn't hear. Maggie shivered for a for a few minutes, then stopped, staring into Magedena's eyes. "I'm sorry", Magadena said softly to her. "You will help the girl? She asked. Maggie sighed, and nodded her head. "I'll see you in time", Magadena said, kissing Maggie on her her forehead. Maggie looked at her, almost ready to break out in a torrent of tears. "What was that? Angelica asked Maggie. Maggie merely shrugged. "We are going back to the pad, and wait for that sonofabitch to come back". Maggie concluded, "This will be the last time you'll have to be afraid". Angelica gave her a puzzled look. She shrugged it off. Maggie was her friend, and she knew what was best. They sat in Jumbo's house, drinking some of his best scotch, right out of the bottle. They cursed him, and giggled. Angelica reached over and kissed Maggie full on the lips. Maggie was startled! Angelica began taking off her clothes. "Are you sure baby? Maggie asked in a horse voice, aroused. "Oh, yes", Angelica moaned. When they were both naked, they climbed into bed, and made love, slowly and gently. They explored each other. It was so different then the rough, eager men Angelica had been with. She felt good, as they finished, and got dressed. It was late at night, when they heard the apartment door open. "Where are you bitches! Jumbo roared. The two walked towards him smiling. Maggie had a pair of sharp scissors behind her back. "How about a hug honey", she smiled sweetly at him. Surprised, Jumbo agreed, putting his huge arms around her. "My number one", he said to her. "Well, you're a number two, asshole! She screamed into his face. Plunging the scissors into his neck. Jumbo yelled in pain, gripping Maggie into a death hug. Maggie drove the scissors deeper into his neck. Blood splattered the both of them, as they slipped, and fell to the floor. Maggie squirmed, trying to get free from Jumbo's deadly grip. Angelica could here Maggie's back cracking, like fire from a furnace. Angelica screamed! Looking around, she spied a kitchen knife, with a ten inch blade, hanging on the wall. She raced to it, grabbing it. She ran back to the battling two. Maggie was grunting, blood spurting out in torrents from her mouth. She still hung on, twisting the scissors deep into Jumbos' neck. Jumbo grunted twice. Blood spilling out on both of them. Of them. Angelica, letting out a scream of anger, plunged the knife several times in the back of Jumbo's neck. Jumbo surprising despite his wounds, jumped up, snarling at Angelica. 'your next, you little whore", he roared at her. He was facing her, his arms reaching out for her. Angelica dropped, and skidded on her bottom towards his legs. She buried the blade deep into his groin. Jumbo screamed in a high pitch, then fell to the floor. Angelica sitting next to him continued her assault on his groin. He laid still, his hands gripped into fists of anger. She pulled out the scissors from his neck. And plunged it into his eyes, squirting out his eyeballs, and blood. She continued her onslaught. "Die you fat bastard! she screamed at him. Jumbo lay still, then filled his pants, the odor of feces filling the air, mixed with blood, and urine. Angelica satisfied he was dead, moved over to Maggie. "God! Angelica thought, she was so still on the floor. She lifted Maggie's head blood poured out her mouth, as she spoke, between blood spurts. "It's alright baby". "We'll be together, soon". Then, smiling, Maggie closed her eyes, and stopped breathing. She was dead! Angelica cried, and then gently closed Maggie's eyes. Angelica cried for hours, her tears resting upon Maggie's body. Then she got a sheet from the bed, and covered her up. "Love you always", she said quietly to Maggie's body. Then she got up, and went looking for Jumbos' secret stash of money, and drugs. She found a plastic baggie, and a drug kit for shooting up, grabbing the stash, she bolted out the door. She was dressed only in her tank top and mini-skirt. Angelica hit the streets, carrying Jumbos' cell phone with her. She dialed 911. She said, "There has been two murders at 1608 oak, hurry! Before the operator could reply, Angelica hung up the phone, stepped on it several times, and tossed it into a nearby dumpster. Soon as in most cases, the money runs out quickly for an addict. After spending it on high priced motels, and drugs, Angelica found herself back on the streets again, giving ten dollar blowjobs, to middle aged men. Her addiction had continually increased, n now strung out, in her filthy clothes, all respect for her had left. She sat in an alley, shooting up her last dime bag. Her mind drifted away calmly, and she began to nod out. She daydreamed of Maggie, remembering her gentile touch, and soft lips. Footsteps were heard trotting towards her. Dreamily, she looked up. A man, probably in his forties, neatly dressed, spoke to her. "How about a little action? He asked her. Sighing, she got up, and knelt down on her knees, slowly unzipping the man's trousers. The man grasped her head firmly. He then quickly with one hand, the other still holding her head, produced a small piece of cloth. He covered her mouth with it. What the hell, she thought, trying to pull away. A funny, overpowering smell emitted from the cloth, invading her nose. Angelica struggled weakly, but the drugs had slowed her reflexes down. She tried to gasp, and then passed out on the ground. The man smiled, picking her limp form up in his arms. He glanced around. Only a homeless man was looking out from his cardboard home, staring at him. "My daughter," the man said, "Going to take her to a rehab! The homeless guy just shrugged and thought, Is that why you were getting ready for a blowjob! Bullshit! But the homeless man kept quiet. Nobody would believe him, and besides, the other man had a dangerous, insane look in his eyes.

The man carried her quickly back to his black van parked outside the alley. 'I think you'll do", the man called Sirocco said to the unconscious girl. He tossed her into the back of the van. No one will miss this bitch! He thought to himself. He climbed into his van, driving away, humming some unknown tune,

# Chapter Seven

Annie woke up first. Yawning and stretching, she rose up from the bed. Looking around, she spied the clock on the night stand next to her. Only seven P.M.! Wow! She thought, they'd really slept a long time! Annie looked at Billy fondly. He was sleeping like a baby, curled up in bed. I could get use to this, she thought, amazed at herself. She had always lived alone, with few boyfriends who came and went frequently. Being a cop, her views on things had probably pissed them off, or scared them. Annie's personality was sometimes abrasive. Guess I'll have to tone it down a little, she reflected. I think I'm in love with Billy, she frowned. Then she smiled. Maybe it will all work out. Thinking this, she smiled, stripping off what she had on, and got into the shower. The scent of their love making was strong, and sweet. She showered slowly, enjoying the warmth on her. After the shower, she stepped out, dried herself off, and went to wake Billy. Billy opened his eyes. "Hi sexy", he said, half awake. His eyes opened wide, seeing she was naked. He grinned at her. "Are you going to get up? She asked. I think I already am", he grinned sheepishly, pulling back his sheet to reveal his erection. Annie smiled, and crawled into bed with him. Annie sighed, Oh well, I'll guess I have to shower again. They made love slowly, and then Annie rested on Billy's chest. Billy grinned, getting up naked, 'I'll fix us something to eat, he said, plodding into the kitchen on his bare feet. Annie followed him, saying "Showers first". "O.k. Billy said, returning to the bedroom. They played around in the shower for a little time. Then they got out drying off. "Time to eat", he said, and trotted off to the kitchen, Annie silently admired his butt. Annie got dressed. Billy cooked them some ham and scrambled eggs. He carried them in on a tray, where Annie sat on the bed. Annie could smell the food. Her mouth watered. When was the last time she ate? Billy sat the tray on the bed. I'll get some coffee here in a minute", Billy told her. "Service with a smile". Annie laughed, surveying his body. "Yes ma'am", he said politely, returning to the kitchen. Billy returned with two steaming mugs of hot coffee in large mugs. "Good, I could use that ", Annie mumbled to him. 'I get I better get dressed", Billy said to her. He looked at her sadly, "Too bad". Annie laughed loudly. Then, she continued devouring her food. Billy got dressed, and then joined her. They ate quietly, and then adjourned into the front room, sitting on the couch. They began comparing notes on the case. "Maybe we'll get an answer at the séance", Annie commented. Shit! Billy said, after everything that has gone on, it can't hurt for sure! Annie just nodded in agreement. They sat their pondering, while Billy turned on the news on the TV. Damn! Annie thought they had gotten a hold on the crimes! They were calling it the Black Magic Murders! Somebody had leaked the story to the press. McCarthy must be shitting a brick by now! The phone rang, declaring to pick it up. "I'm not sure if I want to answer that at all", Billy grimaced. He went over to the table. Picking up the phone. It was Bud's assistant! "Hey Billy ', he said, "I saw it on the news". Billy grunted. Johnny Dugan continued. "Crap's hitting the fan! 'I had a call from Bud, I'm worried". He went on, "He keeps screaming about voices chasing him! 'I asked Victorville sheriffs to go check on him". Oh shit! Thought Billy, that means "Spanky", the sheriff, would investigate. Now Spanky got his nickname as his name was Clarence McFarland, the same last name as the Little Rascals kid. Being only five foot two, and a little chubby, he became a joke on the force, but only behind his back. Spanky had a bad temper, and wasn't beneath assigning one of his deputies to a shit detail for calling himSpanky. Spanky drove furiously, his red lights flashing, to Bud's house, cursing. He hated these welfare checks. But today was boring, so he took the call himself. Probably nothing, but you never new, one time he answered a 911 call, and found a man's wife, trying to saw off her husband's legs. Spanky confronted her, pulling his 40 caliber out. "What the fuck! He exclaimed. The woman, Clare, turned in his direction. "Bastard told me I was a bum fuck, and said dead people moved better than me! Joe, her husband, laid half way on the porch steps, bleeding from his head and blood spurting from his leg. Clare snuck up on Joe, maybe while he was sitting on the porch, and waylaid him while he staggered around the porch. Joe had claimed disability, and stayed drunk most of the time. Spanky knew he had abused Clare for years. This wasn't his first dance with them. Clare held a twelve inch butcher knife, dripping from Joe's blood, flashing it in front of Spanky. "Drop the knife Clare", He said softly, he cocked his pistol. Clare's eyes, rolled around, then glared at him. She screamed at him, as Joe lay moaning in pain, unable to get up, as she had cut through Joe's Achilles tendon. She screamed at Spanky again, advancing towards Spanky. "Fuck you, Spanky, all you men are assholes", she screamed at him, and then charged. "Oh my god! Spanky exclaimed, and then pulled the trigger, firing three shots into Clare. The first one hit her in the chest, spinning her around. The second hit her in the back of the head. It spun her back around again. The third went through her throat, gushing, spurting blood onto the ground. Shaken Spanky approached her prone body. Checking for a pulse. Nothing! Spanky sighed, and then went over to Joe. Joe's eyes wide, and in pain, began mumbling thanks to him. "I think you deserved it Joe", Spanky said, putting away his gun. Spanky called for an ambulance, and then attempted to stop Joe's bleeding. Shaking his head, Spanky drove up to Bud's house. Earlier Bud sat at his kitchen table, still shaken by his attack. Then he heard a scratching, clawing sound! 'What? Bud wondered. He got up to look. Looking around his sparse front room, he couldn't see anything. The sounds continued. Then Bud looked up to his ceiling. There it was! A translucent image of his wife, grinning down at him. Nude, her long red hair flowing, she gave him an evil grin. "Hi shithead", she said, Lowering herself down to confront him. Her breath smelled foul, like brimstone, and death! Her teeth looked long and sharp, like needles. She spoke, her gravelly voice sounding like a concrete mixer in motion. Shit! Bud thought this can't be real! Her skin glowed a ghastly pale white. "Come to me baby, and I'll cure all your ills. She smiled again, gnashing her teeth, together. She held out her arms to him. Then he noticed, something beginning to flow out her mouth. She laughed, as maggots flew forth from her mouth, cascading onto Bud's dress blue shirt. Bud screamed, running away. The specter followed him, laughing. Bud attempted to run out, but the specter blocked his way, holding out her arms, her fingers resembling a lobsters claws. She reached out to grab his groin. Bud stepped back, almost falling over a chair in the kitchen. He ran up the stairs to the second floor. Bud raced into his bedroom. In his closet was a shirt length of rope, he had used to pull down a broken limb with. He raced out to the top of the stairs, rope in hand. Bud couldn't take it any longer. He wrapped the rope around his neck. He tied the rope to the overhanging light on the ceiling. The specter advanced toward him. Her arms outstretched to claim him. "Fuck you! Bud yelled, and jumped! The rope held tight, then snapped, Bud still choking, hit the bottom of the floor, breaking his neck. Bud lay dying, looking up at the ceiling. The specter drifted down towards him. She stood in front of him. "Thank you", she said in that horrible grating voice, "Now you are mine! Buds' eyes stared in horror, as she gnashed her teeth, spouting out maggots, and bent to enfold him. Spanky cautiously crept to the front door of Bud's house. He entered, pulling out his gun, as a precaution. He looked around, finding Bud lying on the floor. Spanky knelt down to check his pulse. No, he was cold already. It was the horrified look on Bud's face, the eyes bulging, and the mouth in a permanent scream that shook him. Spanky shivered, as he felt a cold breeze rush through him. He swore later that he heard the laughter of a woman, sounding inhuman. Spanky called for the meat wagon, and notified the coroner's office on his police radio. He went outside, shaken, keeping distance from the crime scene, warily looking around. Dugan called Billy back. 'They found Bud dead in his house, hung him! Annie saw the look on Billy's face." What is it? She asked. "Bud hung himself", Billy replied, tersely. Billy observed her reaction. Annie looked shocked, then sad. For all Bud's smart ass remarks, bud wasn't so bad, she thought. Billy heard Dugan sob on the phone. "I have to go get him", he said, "He was my best friend! 'O.k. ", Billy said, we'll be there in an hour". He hung up the phone. Billy quickly explained the situation to Annie. They got up from the couch, and left. They started on their way to Bud's house. "Now what ", Billy mumbled, driving. Annie just shook her head. They arrived, observing the ambulance, its red lights, illuminating the night sky. Spanky's police car sat next to it, and Dugan stood there, a horrifying stare on his face. CSI was going into the house, to collect evidence. Annie and Billy approached Dugan standing nervously by. Dugan saw them, then spoke up. "I'm almost afraid of going in. That weird call Bud gave me about the voices really shook me up". Annie touched Dugan's shoulder lightly. "Its o.k.", Annie said to him. "Bud would want you to take care of it". Dugan nodded, and said sadly, "He was my best friend, "I'll wait till CSI clears, then go in". Billy smiled at him. "We are going to get to the bottom of this". Annie and Billy continued on to Spanky, who stood around his patrol car, with a look of terror on his face. The two detectives had never seen that before on him. "What's up Spank . . . ? I mean Sheriff McFarland", Billy spoke. Spanky looked distracted, ignoring the two. Then he spoke, quietly. "Weirdest shit ever . . . found Bud on the floor dead with rope around his neck. I . . . I felt this cold wind, like the grave". He swallowed hard. "I swear I heard a voice straight from the dead, a female voice, cackling". "I thought that I was losing it". Now I'm not so sure". With that, he became quiet again, staring at the ground. Spanky shook, as if he could still feel the icy cold through him. Annie and Billy glanced at each other. "Uh . . . o.k.'", Annie said. 'Don't believe me", Spanky said, "You know I don't bullshit! One thing Annie and Billy knew, Spanky was the least unimaginative person they knew. McCarthy came roaring up in his car, and got out, looking very grim. He looked very tired, and pissed off. "Just what the fuck is going on? He demanded. Spanky just shrugged, and gave some distance away from them. ""Beats my head flat", Billy commented. McCarthy ran his fingers through his uncombed hair. "Some asshole leaked the crimes to the press! "Wasn't us", Annie said. "They're bringing the body out now" Billy said pointing. All of them turned their heads to the attendants bringing Bud's body out, wrapped in a plastic body bag. "Wait a minute", Billy said, He unzipped the bag, and gazed on Bud's face. The look of absolute terror was frozen on his face. "Damn! Billy exclaimed, that look would give him bad dreams for a long time. Annie looked in, a gasp escaped her throat. "This is very dark magic working here! McCarthy looked pale, as his face began to change from anger to horror. He turned away, mumbling. Spanky refused to look, he already had seen it. Billy carefully zipped the bag shut. "Did Bud seem troubled to you? He asked the two detectives. "Not until he worked on the two recent bodies", Annie spoke up. McCarthy returned, "The chief is already on my ass". You better get a line on this quick! Annie and Billy nodded, "Hopefully in the next 48", Annie replied to him. "He wants action now! McCarthy said, walking away to his car. Shaking his head back and forth. CSi couldn't find any evidence of foul play. It would probably be ruled suicide, but Annie and Billy knew otherwise. They returned to the car, and drove off. Maybe they would here from Magadena soon, when he/she sets up the séance. Magadena was in meditation. He/she tried to remove the negative thoughts out of the mind. The thoughts flew through the mind of the shop owner, fast. Magedena's head spun around, dizilly. Back . . . back to when Magadena was thirteen. The name then was Lester Schmidt. Lester had gone into his sister's room, Laurie, and was trying on his sister's dress, a plaid skirt, with a white chiffon blouse. Then he sat down in front of her vanity mirror, and applied her lipstick, a ruby red, on his lips. Lester got up, admiring his image in the full length mirror on the closet door. Oh, I'm very pretty! He thought. His sister who was three years older than him, kept his secret of wanting to be a woman. When everyone slept, they giggled a lot, they tried on panties, bra, and dresses together. Laurie though it was neat, having a secret sister. Mom would probably understand, but that asshole they had for a stepfather would beat the shit out of him, or worse! While Lester admired himself in the mirror, he was so wrapped up in it; he didn't hear the footsteps coming up the stairs towards him. It was his stepfather, earl. A big hulking man, going bald, mean as hell, and very drunk! He looked in; trying to focus his blood shot eyes, in Laurie's room. Then, he spied, Lester, dressed in female clothes, admiring himself in the mirror. Grinning evilly, he crept into the room, quietly creeping up on Lester. He lurched, grabbing Lester's right arm behind his back tightly. "What the . . . Lester said trying to pull away. "So you want to be a bitch, Huh? Earl said, tighten his grip on Lester. "Stop Earl, you're hurting me! Screamed Lester, trying to pull away. 'If you think that hurts, just wait. Earl pinned Lester to the bed, pulling up his dress, and yanking down his underwear. "I'll show you what it feels like to be a bitch! He growled into Lester's ears. NO! Screamed Lester. Lester heard a zipper go down. Lester knew what was going to happen. He struggled, only to have Earl twist his arm, EVEN TIGHTER, the pain shooting up through his shoulder. Then he felt the pressure of something big enter him. "Uh! Lester moaned. Earl pushed, plunging it further into Lester. Lester felt searing pain rush through his body. He heard a scream! It was Laurie, standing in front of the door, a look of disgust and horror on her face! She ran screaming down the stairs. He heard her cry out. "Mom! Earl is raping Lester! Downstairs, Lester's mom sat drinking scotch on the couch. A tired woman, aged beyond her years, sat staring at Laurie. "What the fuck! She said, jumping up off the couch. "Earl's corn holing Lester! Lester is screaming, blood running down his legs! Lester's mom shook with rage! 'That dirty bastard! I'll kill him! Lester's mom, Julie, reached into the desk next to her. She retrieved a nickel plated

357 magnum from it. She checked the chamber, it was fully loaded. Now, she stumbled up the stairs, half drunk herself. Laurie ran hysterically behind her, crying all the way. Julie emerged into the room. Shocked for a moment at the disgusting scene, she recovered, cocking the pistol. "Get off him! She screamed at him. Earl was grunting away, then said, "I'm not done yet, you stupid cunt! Red anger invaded her face and thoughts. She aimed the pistol at his back. Laurie rushed passed her, jumping on Earl's back. She began pulling at him to get him away. Earl growled at her, and then he was free from Lester. The two rolled on the ground. Earl tried to choke her. Laurie punched him in the nose, drawing blood out of it. Earl stood up, clasping his nose. "You dirty bitch! He yelled at her. He moved toward her again. Three shots, exploded in the air. One took out Earl's right eye, the second in his chest, and the third blew away his groin. He stood for a moment, perplexed, took one step forward, and collapsed right on top of Laurie, still laying there, catching her breath. She pulled his dead body away from her, shaking. She rushed over to Lester, passed up from his trauma. Laurie held him, crying. Julie stood as if hypnotized, and then shook her head. "I . . . I better call the ambulance and the police", She stuttered, lowering her pistol. Laurie continued to hold her brother tightly. As if in a daze, Julie went slowly down the stairs, and dialed the phone. She called the ambulance first, then the police. Her main concern was for her son, not that piece of garbage that lay dead! The ambulance arrived, putting Lester on a gurney, and transported him. Laurie had gotten into the ambulance, seated next to her brother, holding his hand. The police arrived, and after talking to Julie, handcuffed her, and put her in the patrol car. Julie never spoke during the entire ride. Arriving at the police station, they booked her into the jail. Still, she never said anything. The one patrolman turned to his partner, and said, that son of a bitch deserved it! He continued, "I hope they go easy on her". His partner nodded his head solemnly. Depending on what judge she got, you never know. Later on, Julie only spoke up once, asking about her son. She was told he would be o.k., as soon as they sew his injury up. Julie remained mute during the whole trial. The two children couldn't figure out why she didn't defend herself. The trial was over, and Julie got ten years for manslaughter. The two children were sad, and devastated. They were sent to their Aunt Susie, and put in her care. Now Susie, a well known Chiropractor in the next town over, was secretly gay. Her personal life was

discreet, and so was her lover, a lawyer who handled civil and criminal cases. Annette, the lawyer, was interested in Julie's case, and had taken over the case, looking for an out to get Julies' case overturned, or a lesser sentence for her. Annette and Susie met frequently to discuss Julie's case, and to make love, afterwards. Lester and his sister liked them both, and treated them like their second parents. Still dark thoughts were surrounding the two siblings. Laurie, who had trouble sleeping at night, began sneaking out, partying beer drinking and smoking pot. Lester insisted on wearing his sister's outfits to school, panties and bra. The two lovers tried talking to them, but it was like taking to a tree. The two kids were polite enough, but still stubborn. Lester was beaten frequently at school, finally was home schooled. Laurie on the other hand, got wilder, and crazy. After her seventeenth birthday, she ran away with her boyfriend, a tough kid poor, but charming. He was also heavy into pot, and now, speed. They took off on his Harley, she only carrying a backpack with her clothes. Lester stayed until he was eighteen, and then left, working in gay bars. Lester got the idea to start a voodoo shop. The owner and Lester's boyfriend, Roy started up the business. Unfortunately, Roy was twenty five years older, and one day died from a massive heart attack, while taking care of the bar. In grief, Lester helped with the funeral. Roy had a will, and left the bar to Lester. Lester didn't want to be reminded of his lost love. So he sold the bar to the employees. Now with that money, Lester built up his shop, and hired a private eye to look for his sister. In two weeks the detective found her, holed up in a cheap hotel, where the cockroaches were the evening's entertainment, Lester rushed over to her. The manager, a swarthy man in his fifties, regarded Lester with disgust. "Why don't you get her out of here? He said, handing Lester a key. "It stinks up there, and she's behind in her rent". Lester took the key, giving the man a look of distaste, observing his filthy wife beater shirt, once white, but now a grungy brown. Lester crept up the stairs to her room, dreading what he would find! He knocked softly on the door, "Laurie, its Lester", he announced. Nothing! Not a sound! The hair stood up on his neck. Fearing the worst, he tried the doorknob. It was unlocked! He entered, as the smell of death, assailed his nostrils. His head reeled, as he saw, his sister lying on the floor. She looked emaciated. Her face sunken in, her teeth rotted, and missing. Lester held his breath, gagging, and approached her. A syringe still clinging to her veins, some dried blood on the floor. She had lost control of her bowel and bladder also, permeating the already foul air in the room. Flies had gathered around her, circling. Maggots were beginning the death dance over her eyes. Lester vomited on the floor next to her. Getting a grip on himself, Lester looked around, spying a dirty white sheet on the bed. Better than nothing! He thought. He draped her body with it. He touched her swollen hand briefly, and cried. After a while, Lester turned, shut her door quietly, and slowly descended the stairs, towards the manager. The manager sat, smoking a cigar, and looking at a porno mag. Lester approached him. Stuttering, he said, "She . . . she is dead! The manager shown displeasure in his face. "Damn! He exclaimed, that junkie whore is stinking up the place! He continued, his tirade, "it'll take me forever to clean it up! A rush of anger filled Lester's face. Rage that he never had before, even after his trauma, years ago. Always non violent, Lester felt the rage flooding out, spreading to his every muscle. Fists clenched, He reached out with his left, and grabbed the startled manager, balling up his dirty shirt. "Hey, let go, faggot! The manager screamed at him. "Not just yet! Returned Lester, and with his right hand punched him several times in his face, drawing blood from it. Lester gave him a shove, releasing him. The manager staggered, holding his nose. "You broke it, Goddamn you! Lester just grinned. The manager reached for the phone next to him. Lester grabbed him by the throat. "The only call you're going to make is to the ambulance, and the coroner! Lester said between his teeth, gritting, "You'll join them too, he said. The manager gasped. Lester pulled out a straight razor from his dress, "Or you can lose something". The manager swallowed hard, and then nodded his head. The ambulance and the coroner arrived. They put Laurie's body into the body bag. The coroner looked at Lester sympathetically, "We'll do the best we can with her", He said. Lester nodded, gave the manager, holding a hanky to his nose, a look of disgust, then left. Laurie had an expensive funeral, which Lester paid for. Aunt Susie and Annette showed up, expressing their condolences. Susie said to softly to Lester. "Your mama got out two weeks ago". Lester looked surprised. "Can I see her? He asked. "I guess . . . Susie stared, and then hung her head. "What is it? Demanded Lester. "Your mother . . . she didn't assimilate well when she got out". Lester stood transfixed, waiting. Annette chimed in. "Y our mom seemed to get lost, wandering around, and we had to go look for her". Lester gasped. Annette continued, she would wake up in the middle of the night, screaming for hours". "It took a long time to calm her. It took both of us to do it! "Where is she now? he asked. 'Upstate at a mental health institution, a private one", Susie sighed. Susie gave him an address and directions. Lester hurried up to his car, a small compact. Susie and Annette waved to him, as he drove off. Annette turned to Susie, and said "I don't think he'll like what he sees ". Susie looked at her, and then squeezed her hand. 'I know ", she said sadly. It took several hours for Lester to get there. He was dressed elegantly, in a black pant suit, with a white ruffled blouse. His red hair was long, trailing on his shoulders. He entered the main office of the building. The place looked more like a resort, than a mental facility. Lots of oak trees, nicely trimmed, rose bushes surrounded the structure. The exterior of the building was bright, with cheerful colors of blue, and green. Lester smiled, and then approached the receptionist. The receptionist, dressed in a blue blouse, and jeans looked at him. She started for a moment, and then smiled at Lester. 'Can I help you? She asked cheerfully. "I'd like to see my mom, Julie Schmidt" {Lester said quietly. "Oh dear! The girl said, "Let me get Doctor Elias to talk to you". She continued, only she had two visitors, sometimes". "Please have a seat". Lester looked around, spotting a soft leather couch by the door, and sat down. A side door buzzed open, revealing a short stocky man in a long white coat, brushing aside his unruly hair with his fingers. He approached Lester, looking surprised. "You are her son? He asked. "No, a daughter", Lester replied. 'Sorry, he said, apologetically. "This way", He said, pointing to the door he came out of. "Buzz us in", he told the receptionist. Lester heard a beep, and then the door opened. The two entered a long walkway, the walls having a pinkish color to them, the paintings of seascapes and mountains adorning the walls. They arrived at a locked gate. Lester could hear the cacophony of voices behind it. An attendant came to the steel gate. Doctor Elias nodded, and the attendant buzzed them in. Lester steeled himself for a chaotic scene. Many patients were milling around. One, prancing around, a man dressed in white overalls, was approached by a huge hairy bald man, who touched him. "Don't touch me I'm pregnant ", he wailed at the bald man. The doctor moved forward, stepping between the two. "That's enough", the doctor reprimanded the huge man. The huge man smiled, then said, "Sorry doc, just having a little fun". The huge man bowed his head, and shuffled off into a corner. "Sometimes, they get carried away ", the doctor apologized. Lester just shrugged. Several catatonics sat staring into space, out a window. Others were talking to their best friends, themselves! Then Lester spied his mom, sitting at a table, looking downward, mumbling to herself. Lester approached her carefully, not knowing what her reaction would be. He spoke softly to her. "Mama, its Lester". Julie lifted her head up, rubbing her eyes, looking at him. "L . . . Lester", she stuttered. She blinked at him, seeing him in his female form. Then she smiled widely. "You are what you want to be". "I'm going to be your new daughter. I call myself Magadena! "He said proudly. "I'm happy for you", she returned, and then she frowned. "I have something secret to tell you", She said, whispering in his ear. "He comes for me at night! She exclaimed. Lester started in surprise. "Who mama? She whispered to him. "That monster, Earl! He comes to me at night, whispering his evil thoughts to me! He said we all were doomed, and that Laurie was already dead! Tears ran down her face, as she continued, "tell me it's not true, my darling daughter". Lester gulped, and then said quietly, "Its not true mama, Laurie is alive". She grabbed him hugging. "Thank god! I thought I was losing what's left of my marbles! Lester tried to put on a positive face. Now he was extremely troubled. Could it be that Earl has returned to haunt us? Lester carried on. With a positive face. "I wish you the best", she said tearfully.. Telling her of his sex change plans, and his prosperous shop made her smile. Lester hugged her. Her once beautiful hair now tangled in knots, and her body was slowly disappearing into a bag of bones and skin. Lester conferred with her doctor. "She vomits up her food, after eating", the doctor said, the next thing to do is feed her through a tube in her stomach, if she doesn't pull it out! "We also are trying to get her hair done, at the beauty salon here. But your mother is quite resistive". "Whatever it takes", Lester said, writing the doctor a check. "I'll send some more money every month". "Your Aunt and her friend help also". "Very well", the doctor said, "I'll start immediately". Lester left, driving back to his shop. He recalled what his mother said, about Earl. Could it be that his evil, continued, even after death? Lester, now Magadena, consulted his spells and incantations. Magadena searched thoroughly through her books. Magadena found "How to dispel and evil spirit." He read it carefully. Placing garlic around the room would help. Magadena turned down the lights, and lit the white candles on the table. Magadena began, "I call on you, Earl, you evil one, to appear before me, and stand judgment! There was a rush of hot air throughout the room, the candles began to flicker. The heat in the room became increasingly unbearable. Magadena began sweating profusely, and then wiped the sweat from his brow. A black mist began forming at the doorway, shimmering, and shaping itself. The image became sharper, and clearer. There stood the figure of Earl, sneering at him. "What do you want, Faggot? He asked, stepping forward. His shape had solidified, making him vulnerable to spells. "You will pay in hell for what you have done! Magadena exclaimed pointing at him, with his finger. "Oh, really", Earl smirked, stepping forward. He encountered the garlic hanging down loftily from the ceiling. "This shits for pusses", he laughed, grabbing a piece of garlic down, and chewed it. "Damn! He said, spiting it out, "At least you could have gotten a fresh one". He moved closer to Magadena, a menacing look on his face. Magadena began the chant. **"If** *a spirit threatens me in this place, fight water by water*, at this, Magadena revealed a small bottle, containing holy water he had retrieved. Then thrust it on Earl. It began churning, burning a hole in his chest. Earl screamed, moving closer. *"Fire by fire* . . . Magadena spoke, stretching out his right hand. Earl burst into flames, screaming curses at him. Magadena continued, *"Banish its power until the last trace. Let this evil being flee through time and space, he finished.* The flames crept over Earl's entire body. His head flew off, severed by the flame, and landed next to Magadena. The eyes looked at her. "Got your mama any way" it said, then crumbled into dust, leaving a damp smear on the floor. "What.., started Magadena, after hearing his last words? He jumped up to get to his phone, He quickly dialed the hospital. He talked to the receptionist.

The receptionist called the doctor. The doctor grabbed the phone, sounding out of breath. "Hello", he said catching his breath. "Magadena explained to the doctor, worried about his mom. "I'm sorry . . . the doctor began. No! No! Magedena's brain screamed. "There was an incident here just a while ago. "He began again. "Black smoke came rolling in through the doors, causing a major brown out in the building. We began evacuation procedures. "I rushed to your mother's door to get her out. I heard a loud crash, and sounds of a struggle, then nothing! The door was heavily locked from the inside". Several attendants and I finally broke down the door". There was chaos! All the furniture had been turned over. The bed and frame smashed into the wall." In the middle of the room, hung your mother, suspended by her gastric tube around her neck, and tied to a rafter above".

She must have pulled the tube out, and used it as a noose". Blood was everywhere, like she was fighting". Magdalena's knees began to buckle. The doctor finished with "We tried CPR, but it was too late! Magadena passed out on the floor. The last thing heard was the doctor. "Hello! Hello! Anybody there? Magadena had recovered enough to go to the hospital, and arrange for his mother's funeral. Sadly Magadena and his aunt and her friend attended it. A small service near the hills. After the funeral, Magadena talked to them. "Are we cursed? His aunt asked. Magadena pulled out of the pockets of her dress, two evil eyes bracelets. "Wear these, it will protect you! The couple looked at her incredulously. "Please! Magadena pleaded with them. Reluctantly, they accepted. They gave Magadena a fond goodbye, and left. Magadena stood alone, gazing at her mom's grave. "I will not let this happen to anyone else I care about", She whispered to the grave. Then Magadena left. She continued with her sex change operation, first the hormone shots, then the breast implants. He. She would do the rest later, as the money was running low. Magadena felt a little better about his/her self again. The shop prospered. Now it was time to pay back her good luck, helping others. Magadena came out of her trance, He/she felt better, cleansed of all the negativity, which overwhelmed the mind. Magadena started preparing for the séance. She/he set the table up, a nice sturdy oak that was heavy enough not to be moved, or thrown around. Her friend, Harmonia, assisted him/her with setting the chairs up. Harmonia, a Haitian, her jet black hair cascading in curls down to her shoulders. She was in her early twenties, very energetic, had joined up with Magadena as the shop owners, séance partner, which was a plus for Magadena. She was almost as tall as Magadena, wearing her white mages robe. She presented quite a respectful sight. Magadena smiled at her nervously, not knowing what the outcome of this journey might be. Harmonia was Magedena's best student, thoughtful, and serious of her white magic powers. The séance setting would be circular in shape. Magadena spread out a white table cloth covering the table. Harmonia put four candles on the table. Magadena went to a clothes closet, and brought out an Ouija board, and placed it in the center of the table. Harmonia gathered up some sandalwood incense. a and placed them around the four corners of the table, placed in an incense burner, shaped liked the god, Dumballah, the king of all voodoo. The figures were magnificently projected. Thin dark skin, an orange and bandana wrapped around his head. A golden bracelet in circled his right forearm. He had short tight braids in his hair. Dumballah, the serpent god, the symbol of the snake, all powerful, for the good, and evil in both the worlds. Harmonia smiled. And thought someone you didn't want to piss off! It was only ten p.m. Still time to do more meditation. The two sat down on the floor, spreading pillows under them, chanted, and entered a light trance. Annie and Billy sat in his apartment, pondering their appointment with Magadena. "I have a strange premonition about tonight", she said, grasping Billy's hand. "What is it? Billy asked concern in his voice. Annie thought for a moment, then said, "something bad . . . but in the end everything should clear up". "Let's hope so", Billy commented, a worried look creased his brow. Annie grasped his hand tighter, and then kissed him. "W e should leave early", Billy said to her. "In about thirty minutes", she said, "Just hold me tight". Billy and Annie embraced intensely.

Sirocco sat in a deep, dark, funk. Enemies! Enemies surrounded him! He could feel their presence encroaching nearer . . . and nearer! He was considerably worried, his mission might be interrupted. So he called upon Bacalou, chanting for his presence. Erzule, now the Voodoo Child, glared at him. "You will pay for your blasphemous, mortal! She screamed at him. She continued, "You are beneath my contempt! She strived to spit at him, but her mouth was dry, only dripping sputum down her face. Soon, she felt, she would have her chance to get released. She would release the tormented spirit of the girl, who resided in her. She felt strong feelings for her. Her tragic life, and her feelings of loosing someone she loved, was buried deep, inside. Erzule could feel something positive coming her way. And where was her husband Dumballah? Somehow the man and Bacalou were blocking him to find her. Bacalou appeared in a puff of oily, smelling brimstone of black smoke that filled the air. "What is it? He boomed at Sirocco. "I have a plan to rid ourselves of enemies! Sirocco stated, He then whispered quietly to Bacalou. Erzule could not here what he said, but she knew it wasn't good! She tried once more to call upon her husband, her inner voice straining with despair. Then her mind searched for other positive energies near her.

# Chapter Eight

Magadena had drifted along in her trance. She remembered the visit from Armando, the gangster, to her shop. He strolled in, dressed nattily in a blue cotton suit, and tie to match. With his beige slacks, and two hundred dollar shoes, gleaming brightly. Behind him were two men dressed approximately similar. Armano spoke quietly, showing Magadena a poster of a fourteen year old girl, smiling. It was the girl Magadena had met once with Maggie. Maggie and her pimp, that piece of shit, was found dead together. Magadena had figured, they had killed each other, and the girl, Angelica had taken off. Magadena had grieved for Maggie, but knew she was protecting her love, to the death. "Do you know her, questioned Armano in a demanding voice? Magadena just stared at him. "Why?, he/she asked, thinking the girl must be in deep trouble, with the mob. "She is my daughter, my angel", Armano said, several tears forming in his eyes. "Oh", Magadena replied, "I have seen her once". Armano noticed his /her voice. He knew what Magadena was, but stayed polite for his daughters' sake. Johnny, overly eager to impress his boss, stepped forward. He was used to imposing his will on others, because of his size, and crazy looks in his face. "I'll get this faggot to talk", he said, growling at Magadena. "Faggot! Exclaimed, Magadena feeling the insult, his/her face burning with rage! Magadena drew a straight line in the air around his/her self, and then smiled. Johnny reached over the counter, with his huge hands, to grab at him/her. He jerked back; an electric shot ran though his body, causing spasms to start. He hit the floor with a thud! Shocked Armano spoke softly to Magadena. "Sorry about that, he's a little too aggressive! With that, he produced a handkerchief from his breast pocket, and wiped his forehead, now dripping wet. He had felt a small charge of the electricity on him. Magadena merely nodded, placing his/her hands down on the sides of his/her robe. Johnny dazed, but got up slowly from the floor. He stepped far way from Magadena, behind Armano, still shaking his head. "You are a *Strega*", Armano said, in Italian, which meant a witch. Magadena nodded his/her head, understanding his meaning. Armano continued, "My mother was from the old country, and told me about such things". Magadena remarked, "I will place the up there, pointing to a prominent place on the wall. "I humbly thank you", Armano said, bowing courteously. He grabbed Johnny, and told the other man, Diego, to leave with them. As they exited, Armano laughed at Johnny. "We'd better go before she turns you into something unpleasant". Johnny just nodded, and as they left, the tune "Tubular Bells", rang inn their ears. "We're going to scout this whole area", Armano told the two, who merely nodded their acceptance. They got into the vehicle, and left. Magadena sighed, removing the protection spell. God! She thought, "What's going on with that poor girl! Magadena decided to enter a silent prayer for the girl's safety. Magadena shivered, she felt a strange sensation that something evil, and powerful was coming. Armano and The other two prowled the streets, for information. Johnny stopped the car, seeing a hooker standing at the corner, looking bored. She was very thin, long stringy brown hair, wearing a dark tube top, and tight jeans shorts. He got out, and approached her. "Hey sweetie", she smiled, some of her teeth missing, "Want a date? Johnny reached into his back pocket, and pulled out a twenty dollar bill. "How about some info", he said, flashing the bill. "Depends", she replied hoarsely, eyeing him suspiciously. Johnny produced a photo of Angelica. The hooker stared at it. She looked from the photo, to the money he held. Giving out a puff of air, she said, "Yeah, I know this kid. She's on the skids now because of heavy H use". "What? Johnny asked, staring. "She was hooking, and then got so bad on heroin; she went down to skid row here, Giving head at five and sometimes ten, for head. The hooker shook her head. "Poor thing, I'm surprised if she isn't dead". Johnny looked shocked. He flashed the twenty into her face. "Where! He demanded. "Shit! "I don't 'know. "Burt tries Mount Vernon and fifth, that's the bottom, she said, than quickly grabbed the money and shoved it down her shorts. Johnny wasn't going to dive to retrieve it. She smiled, and said sweetly, "Want to have a go, big guy". Johnny turned around, walking away. "Thanks ", he said,

"But I've already had the clap before". The hookers face changed, an angry look at him. "Well fuck you! She said, spitting out curses at him, and then flipping him the finger. Jimmy just laughed, and leaned into the car to talk to Armano.

Johnny didn't want to tell his boss about Angelica. He stalled him, temporarily. Johnny shook his head towards Armano. "She told me to check down skid row, on Fifth and Mount Vernon. Armano glared. "What the hell is she doing there? Johnny just shrugged "Don't know". It was late now, almost eleven o'clock. 'Go on, Armano said, gesturing to Johnny. Johnny drove on, till he reached Mount Vernon. Several cheap hotels, which stated, pay by the hour, for the hookers. Litter was scattered everywhere, making everything look even more depressing. Johnny got out of the car, and spied a homeless man sitting sitting in a cardboard box, mumbling incoherently. "Hey *viegrant*" Johnny hailed the man in Italian. "Huh! Croaked the old man, picking at his skin. He looked totally wasted. Johnny suspected the man had lice, amongst other things. He could be in his fifties, it was hard to tell. They aged quickly out here in the street. His clothes, an old pair of dress pants, and open collared shirt was just shredding from his body. Johnny recoiled, as he could smell the urine and dried feces on the man. Johnny coughed, almost gagging, and tried to keep his distance from him. "Have you seen this girl? He asked the man, producing a photo of Angelica. "ONLY in my dreams", the man said, grinning through his rotting yellow teeth. Johnny reached out with his foot, and kicked the man. "You, *Fanook*", growled Johnny at the man. Then Johnny continued, "Don't be a smart ass! The man grunted, and then held out his right filthy hand. Johnny looked at him, the then said "O.k. ", and reached into his wallet, and produced a ten dollar bill. Johnny held the bill just beyond the man's reach. The man sighed, and blinked, staring at the photo with his blood shot eyes. "Yeah", the man spoke, I've seen her". He continued on, "She sells her pussy on the street here, for money to get drugs". "What's that you say? Johnny asked, in a demanding voice. Johnny reacted out and slapped the the man's face. "Hey! Exclaimed the man, rubbing his face, "I've seen her doing it and shooting up dope in this alley. Johnny speechless, his suspicions confirmed about Angelica, threw the ten dollar bill in the man's face, turned and walked away. "Oh shit", Johnny said, "The boss is going to freak out big time! Johnny approached the car, slowly, trying to figure out how to tell his boss. He leaned into the window, as Armano rolled down the window. "What is it? Armano asked, looking worried. Johnny began, speaking softly to Armano. "She's alive", he began, "And . . . Armano asked. "She has become a *La putah* (whore), selling her *La feca* (Pussy), on the streets. "She has become a most deplorable thing, A *Strega, (drug addict).* Armano stare almost froze Johnny in fear. He knew how volatile his boss could be. Shocked out of his senses, he began to flood tears rolling down his eyes. Embarassed, and respecting the man's privacy, Johnny turned away. Armano began beating his fists mercilessly on the back seat of the car. "Goddamnit! He cried out loud, "It's my entire fault! Armano shook his body all over in grief and rage. The other bodyguard, sat staring straight ahead, not moving, in surprise and fear in his eyes. Johnny hung his head in silence. Johnny said to Armano, apologizing, "We'll get her back" Armano sat quietly for a moment. Then he looked up, and said, "Let's go back to that witches shop," "Maybe he's heard of something! Johnny got in the passenger seat, and told the other guy to drive, returning to Magedena's shop. Magadena and Harmonia were ready for what lay ahead. They heard the sound of a car's engine pull up, and then stop. "They're here", Harmonia said, turning towards her mentor. Magadena went to the front of the shop, to greet them. The chimes of tubular bells rang out, as Billy and Annie entered. "Come with me to the back", he/she said, motioning to the two. "WHO IS THAT? Asked Annie, looking at Harmonia. "A powerful psychic, and my student", Magadena replied. "You two sit on the right" he/she stated, motioning to the chairs at the table. "Harmonia and I will sit here", he/she pointed to the two chairs on the left. As they all got seated, Magadena continued, Harmonia will help guide us through the spirit world". Harmonia smiled at them, hoping it would relax them. They looked pretty tense. Annie smiled back, and nodded her head. Billy spoke up, "I'll believe just about anything now", he pronounced. Harmonia got up, turning the lights down low, and returned to her seat. Magadena leaned over, and lit the candles on the table, giving it an eerie sight in the dim room. "Let us hold hands"< Magadena said, reaching out to Harmonia, who in turn, grasped Annie's right hand. With her left, she clutched Billy's hand in hers. She could feel his hand, beginning to sweat a little. She gave him a gentle smile, hoping it would relax him a little. Billy smiled back, nervously. Here we go! Thought Billy. Magadena and Harmonia began chanting in Haitian, Annie realized. Then the two witches began rocking back and forth, more, and more quickly. Harmonia spoke; her voice became rough and hoarse. "Come to us, Marie Laveau, we beg you humbly to help us". "Please appear! Annie and Billy tensed up. The candles began wafing, as a cold wind assailed them. The candles began to get brighter, almost blinding to the eye. Annie felt an invisible rush of air run through her. It was not unpleasant though. Warm and inviting. The sweet smell of jasmine floated around them. Annie felt a feeling of comfort, and love! She smiled. Magadena began stirring in the chair. He/she began speaking in French, then English, haltingly. "Who calls me . . . from the afterlife, I am Marie Laveau! Billy almost dropped his hand, shocked. Annie held on to it tight. "Don't break the circle", she warned. Billy relaxed a little, still staring at Magadena. Harmonia spoke to the spirit. "W e are your faithful followers. We ask you for help against the evil overshadowing us! A form of yellow mist appeared above Magedena's head. It shimmered, and then began taking a recognizable shape. The head of Marie Laveau appeared, solid in shape. Her features were quite clear. The lustrous black hair, anointed with colorful ribbons and bows, like a rainbow, stood out. "I am here to those who believe! She intoned, her head swirling around in circles above Magedena's head. Harmonia spoke up. "A great evil has fallen on this plane, and we beseech you for your guidance, humbly". The spirit's head stopped turning. She gazed upon the group. Marie closed her eyes. The group waited anxiously. Marie spoke up. 'I see it now", she said grimly. "Someone has dared to entrap our loving spirit, Erzule, in a human body". She continued on, her eyes beginning to blaze red hot, searing the air around her. "How's that possible! Harmonia asked amazement in her eyes. Marie continued, "From the help of a dark hearted bokar, and that evil incarnate, Bacalou! "Harmonia gasped, catching her breath, "Oh no! Its evil will spread relentlessly through our world! Marie appeared to nod her head slightly. Then continued, "I know a way to find them. They hold a helpless mortal girl in captivity, with Erzule trapped in there". She continued, "I will need a little time to do this! The spirit turned its head, glancing at Annie. Before Harmonia could speak, the glass windows around them blew out, shattering sharp shards all around them! A whirl wind blew through a broken window, gathering speed, like some crazy dust devil. Magadena turned his/her head, and saw it coming towards her. And then, a puff of mist, yellow and bright, bounded out of Magadena, and entered Annie's' body. Annie jerked, than stiffened up. Harmonia screamed, and then dropped her grip on Magedena's hand. The whirlwind forcibly jerked Magadena out of the chair. The feet dangling in the air above the table. Magadena jerked spasmodically in the air, than began twirling the body around in circles. It began spinning the body around and around, picking up speed, like some crazy Childs toy. Faster! Faster! And faster! The scene started looking blurred to Billy. Annie sat stiffly, her eyes rolling upward, revealing only the whites of them. She sat there in a trance, unmoving. Harmonies screamed again, filling the air with her terror. Harmonia then froze, unable to move! The blur of the whirlwind and Magadena spun even faster. The whirlwind blew the table close to the wall. Harmonia screamed, coming out of her funk, and dashed towards the door, leaving Billy and Annie alone to face the terror. Then, the whirlwind slowed some, revealing Magedena's blood erupting from her mouth, spraying the room. As Harmonia went to exit the door, she heard a loud crashing sound from behind her. Bottles and vials from the cupboards flew about. Harmonia dashed out the door. She stopped to catch her breath. Coward! She thought, I need to go back! A man stepped out of the shadows. "What . . . she began to say. He placed a cloth over her mouth. It smelled like . . . Chloroform! Harmonia weakly struggled. She gasped twice, smelling the chemical, and then collapsed. Sirocco picked her up, placed her on his shoulder, He threw her into a black van still running near the shop. Magadena continued his, / her death dance, being torn apart like some crazy rag doll! Screaming, the left arm flew off, sailing over Billy's head. Magadena mouth opened in a loud, shrieking scream "Shit" He yelled, pulling his weapon. But what to shoot at! The whirlwind continued to pull apart Magadena. His/ her screams became weaker. The right arm came off, then both legs, which flew past Annie, still sitting motionlessly in her chair. Then Magedena's head flew off, sounding like a piece of duck tape, being ripped. It landed on the table next to Billy. Billy jerked, discharging his weapon, hitting the whirlwind. Nothing! Just bullets flying through thin air, making holes in the wall behind it. The head's eyes opened up, staring at Billy. "Bye, handsome", it said, the lips moving slowly. Then the eyes rolled up, vacant as a deserted alley. Annie's mouth moved slowly, each word pronounced, as if learning a strange language. "Marie Laveau", she gasped, sucking in air, with each syllable. Then she stood up, chanting in halting English. "Evil spirit, remove your presence from this room". I Marie Laveau, banish you from this place! Then she held up her left hand, mumbling in Haitian. The whirlwind paused, as if listening. Then a loud, angry sound emitted from it. It quickly went out of one of the broken windows. Billy could hear something crashing in front. Then only silence in the air. Armano and the two bodyguards arrived, and stepped out of the vehicle. As they entered, the shop, they encountered the place in shambles. Windows smashed, shards scattered about the counter and floors. Books were scattered about the floor, pages pages torn from their covers. Potions in vials, and powders were scattered throughout. "What the fuck! Exclaimed Armano. Then he heard movement in the back room. "Here! Armano said, "This way! The two bodyguards stepped in front of Armano, drawing their weapons, and entered the back room with Armano trailing behind them. Armano stood transfixed at the carnage. He couldn't believe his eyes. Magedena's head lay on the table, t its head displaying a grisly sight. Blood was scattered along the walls, and table, like some crazy abstract painting. The two bodyguards, blanched, almost vomiting. Johnny made the sign of the cross, and mumbled, "Holy Mary. Mother of god! "What the fuck is going on here? Armano asked, staring bewildered. Billy stared back at him, and then said, "Fucked if I know! Then he continued, "Evil in the extreme! Annie was standing staring at the wall, and then turned to Armano. 'Who are you *Blanc*", she asked staring at the three gangsters. She gave the two bodyguards a distasteful look. The two with their guns drawn dropped their weapons, as if they were hot, and scalding. "No violence, there's been enough of that here! "Who is she, and witch? Asked Armano, producing a handkerchief from his pocket, wiping his brow. 'I'm really not sure myself", Billy said, looking at Annie. Where is Annie? He asked. Armano stared at them, a puzzled look on his face. Amie, now Marie replied slowly, in a heavy Haitian accent. "I did not take her soul, she grinned, and "She is safer now with me! Annie/Marie continued, "She wants you to trust me, so we can fight this evil together". Billy stared. Could he really trust this . . . spirit, to give Annie back? The spirit sensed his apprehension. "She loves you, Billy, and will return to you after we have finished the mission! Billy sighed; he had no choice at this point. To end all this, and the safe return of Annie, he had to go along. Billy nodded agreement to Annie? Marie? He was a little confused for the moment. The spirit smiled at him. "You can call me either name, honey", she said, "It's up to you". How the hell did she know that was what he was thinking! She gave him an empathetic look. "No magic, just a good intuition" . . . 'Somebody better tell me what the hell is going on! Armano said, Evil . . . the most vile that ever walks the earth", Annie Marie said looking him in the eye. Billy shook his head in agreement. He introduced himself to Armano. Then he described the events leading up to the present. At first looking in disbelief, After Armano saw the carnage there, he reluctantly agreed with Billy. I came here to get info about my missing daughter", Armano, lamented. The two bodyguards picked up their weapons. Armano nodded at them, and they secured their guns back into their holsters. "Show me a photo of her", Annie/Marie said, holding her hand out. She took the photo gingerly from Armano's hand. She closed her eyes, placing the photo on her forehead. She began chanting in some long forgotten language. She concentrated, searching . . . searching through the mazes of other places in time. She began humming some unusual tune, and then stopped. She opened her eyes, removing the photo from her forehead. "Something is trying to block me from seeing", she began, "But I'll have be able to break it soon! 'I hear two voices, one screaming out in pain, the other was having thoughts of escape". "Is it my daughter one of them? Armano asked, anxiously. "Can't say for sure", Annie/Marie replied, I hear sounds, but not a clear picture yet! "When do you think.., began Armano? Annie/Marie interrupted him, "These things will take some time, but I guarantee we will be successful". "I will . . . call? You when I have located them". Armano was at wits end, so he just nodded agreement, and told his body guards to leave. He paused before leaving. 'Here is my phone number, call me anytime day or night". He handed her a business card which read "Armano's salvage, we pick up, and his phone number. Annie/ Marie nodded, and handed the card to Billy. Armano spread his hands out, in sorrow, and said, "Anything I can do, please call, I am very grateful". Then sadly Armano turned around and left. Annie/Marie turned to Billy; she made sure the three gangsters had departed. 'You know here . . . Billy began. Annie/Marie interrupted his statement. 'Yes", she replied, sounding just a little like Annie. 'We need them to stay out of it; it will only cause more chaos in the long run". Billy heartily agreed. All he needed was those mafia guys to fuck it up. "Now what? He asked her. He was still unsure of how this situation would work out. "Now, she said smiling, "We go back to your place, and form some kind of plan". Billy nodded, and they left the carnage of the shop. They approached the car, and Billy looked at her, to see some reaction to it. "Open the door, and be a gentleman", she smiled at him. Billy looked surprised! "Hey! She reacted to the look on his face, "Annie's memories are part of me too". Billy shrugged, and then opened the door for her. She stepped in, sat down, and put her seat belt on securing it. Billy didn't say a word, but started the car, heading back to his apartment, wondering what was next! Annie/ Marie spoke up, when they arrived. "The dirty bokar has claimed another, Harmonia". Billy sat dumbfounded. "He has claimed her body, female parts and all to restore his dead wife's spirit". "How is that possible? He asked in disbelief. "With the magic from Erzule '. He will force her to do it! She finished with "We will stop this bastard, and his evil cohort, Bacalou". "Who the hell is this Bacalou? Billy asked, as they got out of the car to go inside his apartment. "An evil being who preys on our weaknesses and dark thoughts", she returned. "He hasn't completed taken over the bokar, but soon he will be in human form, to carry out his idea of how the world shall be". At this she shook a little. Sirocco continued on with his black ritual. Fusing the part he had severed from Harmonia. Her upper body and genitalia was perfect. Beautiful. His wife would be pleased at this! The other parts were also placed in perfect order. It was now completed. Soon, he would enjoy her smile, her love, again. Bacalou appeared a horned demon, with grey scaly skin, protruding from him the smell of brimstone and death lingered around him, permeating, filling the air Sirocco gagged a little . . . then composed him. It would be a good idea not to show his disgust that could be a fatal error. Bacalou thought, soon he would take over this stupid man's soul, and bring a wave of hell no mortal could imagine. Then he laughed a loud sinister laugh! It sounded like the dead souls of many, the cacophony echoed throughout the building. Sirocco looked at the evil being puzzled. What the hell was that, he thought. Bacalou just grinned, his mouth opened, his razor sharp teeth exposed. Sirocco gave a quiet shudder. Bacalou thought, when I'm done he would get rid of that bitch, Erzule. Sirocco frowned. When he has returned his wife to the living, he would set Erzule free to deal with Bacalou. Hopefully she would go after Bacalou first, not him. Keeping my fingers crossed, he thought. If she did go after him, he had a plan to return her back into the chained body of the Voodoo child. Sirocco continued studying the body.

Erzule stared at him, straining against the chains that bound her. "Fool", she said to Sirocco, She continued, "Bacalou will enslave you! "Shut up bitch! Sirocco said, "I'll take care of you later! Erzule gritted her teeth. When the moment came, she would take care of them both, with relish! Erzule felt a surge of power coming through her body. Faint, but just enough to reach out for help. She sent a wave of distress out. It was straining her will power, but it was going to work. Patrolman Benita Torres was patrolling nearby. She had responded to reports of strange sounds coming from the old steel factory. The factory had closed ten years old, and nobody seemed in a hurry to buy it. There were rumors of course. Rumors that it was haunted because of several incidents involving deaths of some employees. They were ruled "Accidental", by authorities, but Torres always thought they were not. Rumor had it that some had refused to pay their union dues, to the boss, who was Armano, a known gangster. Make you an offer you can't refuse, thought Torres grimly. Torres was the mother of three small children, whose father had, ran out on them. The bastard! A plumber, he was trying to beat up, Benita when she shot him in the ass, as he was backing off from her. Ed, the asshole screamed like a little girl, and hit the floor. When the police arrived, they talked to her. She explained the situation. Several cops knew her Dan Cooper, a patrolman and friend had seen the bruises on her before. He looked around, and told his partner Chloe, to handcuff Ed up. Ed complained, "Ow! My ass. "I need an ambulance. Chloe sneered at him. "You won't die asshole". She stood him up. "I'll take this one outside, and call for an ambulance". "Hope it's busy, and takes its time! Giving Benita a sympathetic smile, she half dragged Ed outside to the patrol car. Cooper walked over to the kitchen. He found a ten inch butcher knife hanging on the wall. Putting a glove on, he grabbed it and returned to Benita, who was nursing a fat lip, and a black eye, slowing turning darker in color. "He attacked you! He said to her, tossing the blade onto the floor Benita looked up at him, smiling her best, squinting through her bruised eye. The case never went to court. While Ed was in jail, he got beat up twice by a big black man, who wanted to treat Ed like his bitch. When Ed's mother showed up to bail him out, he cried, and grabbed his mother's hand. They left in a hurry. No one saw Ed after that. He just vanished, leaving speculation as to where he went. Most thought his mother, a domineering woman, had moved Ed out of state, to protect him. She knew what would happen if he hung around! Benita deep in her thoughts was suddenly hit with a wave of sound, reverberating in her ears. "Help me! Please! It exploded in her head. Torres stopped the patrol car. She shook her head. Where the hell was that coming from! She was stopped in front of the old steel factory. The emanations became stronger in her head. Then it stopped, as quickly as it came. Torres could still feel that there was a cry for help. She withdrew her weapon, a 380 Sig Sauer, and approached the building slowly. At five foot three, and one hundred ten pounds, she could still hold her own with any perp. She checked the the metal door of the entrance, its hinges rusted away from the weather, the door hanging loosely like some forgotten relic. Torres squeezed her small frame through it, cocking her weapon as she entered. She looked about, trying to make as less noise as possible. She strained her ears, listening for something. Just rusted out factory equipment, sitting there waiting to be used again. Then she heard sounds below, on the lower level. She advanced slowly down the stairs, practically creeping along. The sounds grew louder. Two voices! One that sounding human to her, the other voice, not something she ever heard before, unearthly, guttural spoke louder than the other. Torres leaned forward, trying to hear what they were saying. "OUR mission is almost complete", said the normal voice. Then Torres saw who he was talking to. The hair on her page boy haircut stood up on her neck. What the fuck was that! She stared in disbelief at it. A horned scaly thing with protruding its sharp teeth, resting on its forked tongue! A persons nightmare at least! Then Torres spied the girl. Young, and helplessly bound by chains to her hands. She looked sad and filthy. Disgust rose up in Torres' throat. The girl looked up, seeing Torres on the stairs. She smiled at Torres, and then nodded her head towards the two who were busy in their discussion. Torres advanced along, keeping an eye out for the two, her weapon raised in their direction. She crept up quietly to Erzule. Erzule tensed up, hoping the two men didn't notice. Torres held her finger to her lips, letting her know that Erzule should be quiet. Torres strained to loosen the chains. No way, they were bound tight, around the girl's wrists. She noticed a hole in them, enough for a key. Where the hell was it! Torres thought. Erzule nodded towards a table, about ten yards away from the two men. Torres nodded, slipping quietly away from the girl. She crept slowly towards the table. Just as she reached the key, she stubbed her toe, on something. It was a piece of used metal, left over from the old days of the factory. Goddamn! She thought, looking towards the two men. The ugly thing next to the man raised its head up, growling. Shit! Torres thought, it saw me! Torres grabbed the key, and ran back to the bound girl. "Go away! Save yourself! Screamed the girl. "Not until I get you free". Said Torres stubbornly, fumbling with the key. "Look out, it's coming! Screamed the girl. Torres turned, and saw the beast slowly rambling toward her, licking its lips. The man staring at Torres grinned. "Goodbye", he said. Torres dropped the key, and fumbling again, drew her weapon. Fuck warnings! She thought, emptying the clip into the charging beast. Bacalou laughed, as the bullets went through him, not leaving a trace. Tories looked into the chamber. Empty! She reached down on her belt, recovering her spare clip. She reloaded. Aiming at one of the chains, she fired, freeing Erzule's left hand. As Torres turned to the other chain. To shoot it, the beast grabbed her, roaring in her face. Erzule struggled trying to get her other arm free. Sirocco raced towards them, his hands razed in anger. He jumped into the Malay, trying to grasp the weapon from Torres' hand. Sirocco was in reach of Erzule's left hand. She reached hard down to his groin. Grasping both testicles she twisted them as hard as she could. Sirocco screamed in agony, as she twisted even harder, Bacalou and Torres were face to face. He grabbed her head, squeezing it with all his power; her eyes began popping out of her head. Torres screamed, looking at the beast. "Go fuck yourself! Her final last words spoke, as her head collapsed, like a burst balloon. Bacalou turned his attention to sirocco, still screaming in pain. He forced Erzule's' hand away, snapping her wrist, with a sickening crack, as the fragile bone broke. Erzule yelped in pain. Sirocco fell to the floor, screaming about his balls. Bacalou struck Erzule, hard, almost breaking her neck, as she collapsed. Bacalou looked down at the lifeless body of Torres. Brave officer, mother of three. "I'm going to eat your soul", he pronounced loudly, reaching down for her dead body. Erzule came to at that moment. "No way! She screamed at him. She moved her hand, her wrist aching in pain, and pointed down at the dead woman. "Brave soul. You are committed to the world of Nirvana now! As she spoke a mist of colorful array, rose up, and vanished upwards. "Damn you! Bacalou yelled at her. Then he struck her harder again, this time knocking her out. She collapsed, with a dignified smile. Sirocco regained himself from the floor, tears in his eyes. "The fucking bitch, I'll take care of you." Sirocco wrapped another chain around the left wrist of

Erzule, making it so tight, her wrists bled a little. She came to in agonizing pain. Tears filled her eyes. She glared at him. "Awake huh", Sirocco said smugly. He then slapped her face twice, leaving a rash of red marks on it. He reached over and squeezed her left nipple hard, bringing even more tears in her eyes. They were filled with pain. He twisted a little longer, and then released his grip. She spat at him, tasting blood in her mouth. Sirocco laughed, and then walked away. "I want to have her after were done", Bacalou growled at him. 'She's `yours, after", Sirocco said, then rubbed his groin." Hurts huh! Bacalou grinned. He continued, "Need a massage", he said, snapping his clawed hands together. "I'll get over `it", retorted Sirocco, shaking his head, and turning away from him. More work to do before the blood moon rises in three days. He wanted everything perfect then!

# Chapter Nine

Billy and Annie, now Marie? Arrived at his place. Plodding up the stairs, to his apartment. As they entered, she asked, "Is this your abode? "Yes Billy replied, "What do you think? Annie, now Marie replied, "I love it! All this is so new, and exciting to me! Billy sat down in the couch, and Annie/Marie sat next to him. She put her hand on Billy's thigh. Billy fidgeted nervously. She laughed, then said, "Its o.k. Blanc, I'm not going to do anything . . . for now! She gave him a wide grin. Billy cleared his throat. "Where is this ritual going to happen? He asked. "I'll know it when I see it, "she replied. "It's somewhere in the northern part of the city. Unclear yet, it will come to me soon: Billy's eyes began getting heavy. "I need to get some rest", he said yawning. "Good idea", she said. Billy could see something in her eyes. Probably lust! She hasn't been physical with a man for what . . . two hundred years! Billy swallowed hard. "In there, you can have the bed, and I'll take the couch. She smiled, that sweet Annie smile at him. Damn! he thought. "You sure", she asked, her voice sounding low and sexy. "Uh uh . . . yes, he stuttered, his face blushing a little. "All right", she said, looking him over, "but if you change your mind, let me know". She walked slowly towards the bedroom, rolling her hips suggestively at him. Graceful, and extremely sexy, just like Annie. "Damn her", he said to himself, feeling frustrated. He then took off his clothes, and clad only in his boxers, fell asleep on the couch. His dreams were filled with sex, and sometimes violent, as he drifted along. Armano and his two bodyguards were on the move. Knocking down doors in the shady streets, he had found out about Angelicas boyfriend, a well known pimp, and dope dealer. They drove to his pad, to see him. It was two A.m. in the morning. The sky was filled with darkness, hiding its sins away there. The three arrived, got out, and then got out. They stealthily approached the front door. Everything was quiet. Slowly, Johnny turned the door knob. It was unlocked! Good! Johnny and the other drew their weapons as Armano stood behind them. They entered, scouting around the front room. Largo lay naked, sprawled on the couch, with two big busted blondes lying beside them. Drugs were scattered on the table, and even the lush gold carpet there. Jonny stepped over, a look of disgust spreading on his face. He despised people who couldn't control themselves, and their urges. Johnny reached out and slapped Largo hard with his huge hand, making Largo come to, staring at Johnny. "What the fuck! He said jumping up. Johnny backhanded him again, forcing Largo back down on the couch. Largo blinked, tears in his eyes, stunned for the moment. "Who the hell are you? Largo demanded, asking. 'Your worst nightmare, motherfucker! Johnny growled at him. Armano stepped up to were Johnny stood. "Do you know who I am? Armano asked quietly. 'An ugly wop", said Largo defiantly. Johnny leaned over, and this time, punched largo in the mouth. Blood spurted out, like a squeezed ketchup bottle. "Shit! Largo yelled, holding a hand over his face, trying to wipe the blood off. "Yeah . . . Largo stammered, your Angelica's father. Largo grinned, "She was a tight piece of Ass". Armano's face grew dark dark with anger. "Get me a pair of pliers", He said to Johnny. Johnny went looking through the kitchen. He returned with a large robo grip pliers. 'Hold him down! Commanded Armano! The two grabbed his arms pinning him to the couch. The naked girl woke up, staring at the three. One looked at Armano. 'You bitches get out now! He said to them. The one girl shook her friend, her eyes bulging out at the sight. They got up, grabbing their clothes on the floor, and ran out naked, fumbling to get their clothes on. "Now where were we? Armano asked. He took the pliers from Johnny adjusted the width, and clamped them hard on Largo's testicles. Sweat poured out on Largo's forehead. "What did you say about my precious daughter? Armano asked, almost gracessly. He clamped down hard with the pliers on Largo. Largo opened his his mouth to scream. "You scream like a sissy lala, and Ill sqeeze your nuts off., Armano said, grinning. Largo shut his mouth, his body tense with pain. Then Largo spoke, I'm sorry, "he said, gritting his teeth. "Where is she? Armano asked, turning the pliers a quarter turn. Perfuse sweat mingled with blood flowed from him to the floor. "For gods' sake! He cried out in pain. "I . . . I gave her to Jumbo the pimp. After that I don't know! He moaned loudly. Armano was given directions to the pimp's house. "There there! Armano said soothingly. "Isn't it better for the soul to confess"? He removed the pliers from Largo's groin. Largo sighed in relief. Armano nodded to Johnny and the other one. They released Largo from their grip. Largo sat shivering, head down, crying. 'Were all done here now", he said to the two. He nodded towards Johnny. Johnny pulled his gun, discharging it at largo. The first shot took Largo's testicles away. The second shot went through Largo's right eye. Largo jumped up, a look of shock on his face, and then collapsed in a heap on the floor. "You scream like a pussy", Johnny said to the body. I've tortured women who were tougher than you, scumbag! Johnny spit on the dead body. Holstered his weapon, and went out the door with the others. Billy was dreaming, when he felt someone straddling him. Then groping his genitals. "Annie? He asked half awake. Two gentle hands slipped off his boxers, and began manipulating him. Billy could feel his hardness growing. He felt something warm, and wet clutching his groin. Billy gasped! It was Annie, but not Annie. It was also Marie Laveau. "Wait,. I can't ", moaned Billy, as Annie? Marie, began thrusted her hips back and forth on him. She produced a necklace, from behind her back. The damn slave necklace! She looped it around his neck. Billy felt his will power diminishing away, and enjoying the moment! Annie/Marie moaned, she said "Sorry Blanc it's been too long for me". She moved her hips again, in a slow, steady rhythm. Moaning louder, she whispered, "It's still Annie's body". She groaned. "She agreed to this when I entered her. Billy looked at her surprised. A look of lust filled her eyes. She started moving her hips faster . . . and faster. Billy felt himself about to erupt. Annie/Marie and Billy yelled out in climax. 'Damn he thought, hating to admit it that was good! Annie/Marie bent down to kiss him. Then she slid off him, standing there, naked, smiling greatly at him. She said, "I think I need to bathe now, honey". She turned away, and headed towards the bathroom. Billy followed her, showing her how the shower worked. "I know this", she retorted, "I have Annie's memories with me". "Nice", she murmured, as she enjoyed the jet spray of warm water. Billy retrieved some towels for her, and left to go into the front room. Billy sat down at a table in the kitchen. He began taking his weapon apart. Realizing he was naked, he got up, went into the bedroom, and put on jeans, and a grey t-shirt. He returned to the table, and pulling out some gun oil, he began to clean his weapon. After cleaning the inside, he began reassembling it. It took him about ten minutes to complete the task. Annie/Marie emerged from the bathroom, her hair wrapped up in a towel, another around her body. "Cleaning my weapon ", he remarked to her. "Annie has shown me that', she said, sitting down at the table, crossing her legs. "Good", Billy said, "get yours and clean it". Getting up she went into the other room, returning with her nine millimeter pistol. She sat down at the table. She disassembled, cleaned, and put the weapon back together. In five minutes! Billy was impressed. Now he knew he could count on her in a clinch. The phone rang urgently. Damn! Billy thought, wonder who that is. Billy reluctantly answered it. It was McCarthy! "You need to get over to that charm shop, you went to", He paused. "There's a hell of a mess down here". Evidently a customer entered the shop, and made a grisly discovery! Screaming at the top of her lungs, Dory, who was a regular there, went running out to the street, alerting other shop owners to step out, to see what was going on. "It's a goddamn mess! Exclaimed McCarthy, over the phone. "We'll be there", Billy said, hanging up the phone. "What? Asked Annie/Marie, seeing the funny look on Billy. Someone gas found the scene at Magedena's shop. "We have to show up, like we don't know what happened! "Well alright, Blanc, whatever you say". With that, she got up from the table, tossed off her towels, and stepped naked into the bedroom. Billy admired her, and then thought, I wish she wouldn't do that! After Annie got dressed, Billy got dressed. Then they left to the crime scene. Driving along, Annie commented on how she enjoyed the ride. Billy just smiled, when a blue SUV, cut him off in traffic! Billy could hear the boom, boom, bass of the resounding sound of rap, loud, and obnoxious. "Fucking assholes! Billy yelled out the window. There were three black teenagers, inside, laughing at them. They pulled over, maneuvering next to Billy's car. Annie. Marie turned her head to glare at them. "How rude! She exclaimed angrily. She continued, asking Billy, "What's that insane noise? Billy grunted. "They think that's music". "Not in this world or the next", she pronounced. She scooted closer, almost sitting in his lap. "What . . . Billy began. She placed a finger against her lips. Billy concentrated on his driving. The two cars were almost touching, side by side. He was hoping no traffic would come from the other direction, obliterating them. Annie/ Marie leaned out the window as far as she could go, almost blocking Billy's vision. Her eyes began glaring red hot. Billy could feel the heat emanating from then. He started to sweat profusely. Wiping the perspiration from his eyes, he continued concentrating on the road. "Hey mama! The teenager in the back seat yelled at her, "Let me tap that ass", he grinned at her. Annie/Marie blew him a kiss, and then made circular motions with right hand. She mumbled some strange words at the other vehicle, perhaps in Haitian. Then pointed a finger directly at them. The hood of the SUV, buckled, and then exploded in the air, sending shards of metal behind them. It completely obscures the SUV's vision of the driver. Annie/ Marie and Billy heard the driver cursing. The driver pulled over to the shoulder of the road, almost hitting a highway sign next to it. Billy looked at her, and then laughed out loud. "So? She asked. "'The frustrated motorists greatest dream". She smiled wide at him, and Billy returned it even wider. They drove away, a look of happiness on both their faces. They arrived moments later, still smiling about the incident as they saw the driver cursing at them, as they drove off. Their smiles turned grim as they approached the shop. McCarthy stood at the entrance, looking visibly shaken. The assistant coroner stepped out from the shop. He looked a little green in his face, like he wanted to vomit. Two ambulance attendants stood by. A CSI team arrived, and entered the shop, with a gurney and body bag. Billy hollered at McCarthy. "Hey, boss! He hollered at him. McCarthy looking pale looked at the two. "Sweet Mother of god! He said. "Do you know anything about this? Billy and Annie/Marie looked at him, acting surprised. McCarthy looked tired, bags under his eyes, looking for a long extended vacation. The two, stepped up to where their boss, stood, his head shaking slowly back and forth. "Have you gone in yet? Billy asked him. Unfortunately", McCarthy said this time quietly. "I was hoping you two would go back in there with me ", he said, still looking disturbed. The three entered the shop. Chaos! Bottles, powders in glass vials, thrown about, and shattered. The scene of intense anger and hate. Annie/Marie smelled the air. Yes, she thought, an evil spirit still lingers prevailing the room. She mumbled something in Haitian under her breath. The foulness of evil disappeared throughout the air. Satisfied, she looked to Billy. Then the three smelled it! The rancid decaying odor of decomp. McCarthy gagged, Billy turned away from it, and Annie produced a small handkerchief and placed it over her mouth and nose. "Holy shit! Billy commented, turning back towards the pungent smell. They stepped into the back room. The ambulance team was placing parts into a body bag. The smell was overpowering. "we had to scrape some of it off the wall', the youngest attendant said, grimly. The older one produced a small container of cream from his pocket. "Noxzema", he said bluntly, handing it to McCarthy. "Put some in your noses, it helps kill some of the smell. All three did so, and then handed it back to the older attendant. "I've seen some bad crap in my time, but this . . . this takes it all! He concluded, zipping up the body bag, with a final zip! Then put it on a gurney. The three stared. The images would stick in their minds for quite some time. As the attendants were cleaning up, they had seen a severed leg on the floor, and arm was plastered to the table, as if it was glued there. The torso sat straight up, as if greeting them. Magedena's skull rested on top of the table, along with his/her breasts. McCarthy rolled his eyes. His legs bended, almost to the point of collapsing. Being a somewhat professional, he pulled himself together. Billy looked at Annie/Marie, and nodded. Annie/ Marie slipped out, to see if she could find some sort of protection for them. Annie/Marie looked around, sorting through the maze of broken bottles, and vials. She looked through the remaining elements on the shelve, that hadn't been destroyed. Looking above the cupboards, she saw lettering, in blood on it. It was printed in ancient Sumerian. *Hal Hal —am* it read. (Kill, murder). And below that was *Adila, basi, alako(to bring to naught)*. A warning! She shook her head, and continued looking for the charms that were needed. McCarthy asked, Billy, "Can you explain any of this? Billy hesitated, choosing his words very carefully. 'Looks like some black magic gone bad". "When's this shit ever going to stop? McCarthy asked, and then lapsed into mumbling. McCarthy let out a long sigh. Billy looked at him, and trying to sound at least some confidence, said, 'Soon, we have some leads". Billy explained to him he may have a lead. And determined, he thought to leave out the séance bit. He was afraid his boss would go into max overload, if he really told him. The CSI, a young redheaded female, named Janie stuck her head in. "Craziest shit I've ever seen! Looks like a tornado flew through here. And . . . she paused, no latent prints worth collecting! "How is that possible? McCarthy asked, as the attendants carried out the remains of the victim. Annie had returned, carrying a small plastic evidence bag in her hand. "What's that? Asked McCarthy, pointing at it. "Some evidence we need," she said imitating Annie's voice pitch perfect. "Be sure you turn that in", McCarthy said, ignoring the body being carried out.

'You bet", returned Annie/Marie, touching Billy's arm, a sign to leave now. "I'll call you when something breaks", Billy said to his boss, then the two left, leaving McCarthy boss, then the two left, leaving McCarthy mumbling to himself. Armano had arrived at Jumbo's. The crime scene tape falling apart around the house. Armano Looked around. What the hell happened here? He surveyed the area. A young man in his twenties rode by, pedaling slowly. Armano stepped in front of him. The youngster skidding to a stop. He regarded Armano warily. "What's the dealio, dad", he asked, a smirk on his face. Armano opened his jacket to reveal a 357 magnum, gleaming at the cyclist. "This is the deal, punk, Armano began, a grin on his face. He continued, "If you get the answer to my question, you get to live, and get twenty bucks for your trouble. If not . . . Armano said, showing the cyclist his weapon again. The young man swallowed hard, and then spoke up. 'WH . . . What do you want to know? The cyclist stood on his bike, his fingers moving frantically on the handlebars. "Relax, kid", Armano said, closing his jacket. Armano continued, "Have you seen her? He asked, producing a photo of his daughter. The young man looked intently at it. It could be his death, if he answered wrong. "Yes . . . I've seen her before". "Where! Here! When! Armano demanded, taking back the photo. "She's one of his hookers', he began. Armano gave him a dirty look. "Sorry", the cyclist apologized. "Go on", urged Armano. "She left several weeks ago". He continued on. "There were two murders in that house! Jumbo and his number one girl, Maggie killed each other". And the girl? Asked Armano, apprehensively. "I think she ran off", the cyclist finished. "Well she's still alive", commented Armano, pulling a twenty out of his wallet, handing it to the young man. The cyclist nodded, and proceeded to ride off. The cyclist turned back to Armano, who stood, with his head down. Breathing a sigh of relief, the cyclist pedaled off quickly, before the scary guy could change his mind. Armano had no idea where she could be. He had to take a leap of faith, to assume what the female cop had said. There was something odd about her. He couldn't quite put his finger on it. Something dangerous, and unpredictable! She was the one to watch, alright! Armano gestured at his two bodyguards and left. They returned to his house. Armano was exhausted. He told his two shadows to get some rest, as he was going to. Armano posted two others to guard the house while they rested, Armano drifted into sleep. His mind still troubled about the events that had occurred, His dreams carried on in a maze of thoughts. The revelation of what Angelica had become! The death of the witch at the shop! The deaths of the pimp and his girl. The idea that his sweet Angel had become an instrument of this somehow. Angelica's face came to him. Her lips moved slowly, as she said . . . "Daddy, I won't forgive you for Uncle Tony, but you still are my only parent! Mist swirled around her face, clinging to her image. "I am in danger! "Please listen to the woman cop, she is the key! Another face appeared, shining brightly at him. "She is out of your reach, for now! The face gained shape, shimmering in the mist. "Beware! She is safe for now. "Only tragedy will follow. "The face was dark skinned, yet revealing power behind it. Armano awoke; sweat pouring out of him, descending on his pillow, damp from him. Armano visibly shaken, got up, and poured a shot of whiskey. He downed it quickly, and then returned to bed. This time, he slept dreamlessly.

# Chapter Ten

Annie and Billy had returned to his place. Trotting up the stairs, Billy was anxious to see what Annie/Marie had brought back to the shop. They entered and both sat down at the table. Annie opened the clear plastic bag; she pulled out several unknown objects from it. "What the hell is that", Billy said wrinkling his noise. "Oh, the good stuff", she murmured. "Like what? He said, looking at the objects in distaste. "For protection for both of us". She continued, "Some horseradish, a couple of coffin nails! She held them up to Billy's face. Billy leaned back from the offending odor. Annnie/Marie laughed. "You don't have to eat it". "Good thing to! Billy retorted, "I've had enough problems with my stomach! Annie laughed again. Then she got serious. "It will give us some minimal protection". "And the rest? Billy asked. 'That would be up to me, and Erzule, when I free her". "Hopefully . . . Billy said, pausing. "It will all work out", she said, "But sometimes there will be a price for it! "Like what? Billy asked, beginning to wonder. 'It's unknown", she commented, "Sometimes a small price, sometimes a big sacrifice! Billy pondered this for a moment. Annie/Marie merely shrugged her shoulders. "I'm going to meditate on this for a while", she said, going off to the bedroom. Billy felt tired, and decided to take a short nap, to iron everything out in his mind. Annie/ Marie sat cross legged on the bed. Closing her eyes, she began slowly chanting in her native Haitian tongue. Billy drifted into a deep, dark sleep, filled with dangers of demons, and monsters chasing him. He tossed and turned, on the couch. Somewhere, in the back of his mind, he heard Annie/Marie chanting. **"Dumballah, Dumballah"**, help your faithful servant in time of need! "Your beloved is trapped in our world by an evil spirit, and desperate man! "I beseech you humbly! There came a loud noise, as if a 4.1 earthquake shook the apartment. Billy woke with a start, jumped up to look around. The sound was coming from the bedroom. He grabbed his weapon, and rushed into the bedroom, not knowing what to expect. There Annie/ Marie sitting on the bed, A swirling opaque mist hovered in front of her. She was chanting to it. Clanging noises erupted through it! "Dumballah, Dumballah", she chanted. The mist cleared, she continued, "Come help your lost love, Erzule". After the mist cleared, revealed a dark skinned man, almost eight feet tall, standing at the bottom of the bed. He was brightly covered in a lavender headdress, Adorned in multi—colored flowers. His eyes glowed brightly red, like some streetlights, only twice as bright! His voice boomed, rattling the bedroom windows. "Who dares to entrap my love! "An evil Bokar", she replied, looking at him in awe. She continued "that man has dared to invoke that evil one, Bokar, your greatest nemesis". A horrendous growl came from his throat. "What mortal fool dares raise the evil one? He spat out, anger in his voice. She replied, "A desperate man, trying to recover his wife's spirit into another". "This is not the way to do things! He shouted, shaking the walls. He continued, "He should have called on me! She replied to him, His heart has become dark, and Bacalou encourages it! She continued, "Soon, he will eat the man's soul, and take over his body". "This I cannot allow! He said, more quietly, "But somehow Bacalou is blocking my vision, to where they are at! "Leave it to me", she said. "I will find out, and call to you to help". "Very well, I trust you", he said, then vanished into air, not leaving a trace. Billy stood in the doorway, his mouth opened in shock. "What the hell was that? He exclaimed. 'Help we sorely need", she replied. She continued, "Hey! She said, "I'm hungry, let's get something to eat! Billy stared at her in amazement. After that scene with that . . . sprit, she acted like it was a normal occurrence. "Sure, what the hell", he said. They left, Billy still shaking his head. Billy was still dumbfounded, and did not notice a suspicious looking SUV, parked across the street. Armano, Johnny, and the other bodyguard, watched the two drive off. Armano leaned forward to Johnny in the front passenger seat. "Let's wait for a while; to be sure they're gone". Johnny nodded in agreement. They waited for fifteen minutes. Then Armano said, "Go plant the bug in the apartment now. "Be careful". Johnny just nodded, and then left the SUV, the electronic bug, a listening device, clutched in his right hand; He crept slowly up the stairs, to Billy's apartment. As he reached the apartment he stopped, listening to any sounds from the other apartments, He could only hear loud music blaring in the next room to Billy. Shrugging, Johnny reached into his left trouser pocket, and produced a lock pick. Johnny began fumbling with it. Click! The door opened. He heard a door slightly open, and then close. He looked around, but saw nothing. Must be my nerves! He thought, pushing the door open, and stepping in. He glanced around, looking for a good spot to plant the bug! Ah! He thought, under the coffee table, no one looks under there. Johnny took the bug, with some adhesive tape he found, and placed it securely there. He stopped before exiting, listening for any unusual sounds. Nothing but the loud music next door. They probably couldn't hear a gunshot at that volume! Johnny smiling exited the apartment quietly, then relocking the door. As he left, he didn't see a face peer out of the curtains, watching him. Billy and Annie/Marie ate quietly, then he paid the bill, and they left returning to the apartment. Johnny got into the vehicle." All set? Asked Armano. "Yep, ready to go", Johnny replied, grinning. He handed Armano an earpiece to listen in. They watched as the two detectives climbed up the stairs to the apartment. Billy paused for a moment, getting his key out. He could hear the boom, boom, of heavy metal next door. Annie/Marie commented, "What the hell is that? Billy grinned, 'The head banger next door. ". "What she thinks is music". Annie/Marie made a face. 'Do you want it stopped? She asked seriously. Billy held up a hand. "No! He replied. "I'll take care of it! He banged on the door as loud as he could. It took a few minutes, but the curtains to the other apartment opened. A young girl peered out between them. Billy flashed his badge at her. The curtains closed, and he heard a voice, which turned the music down. I'll be just a minute", she said. Billy could hear some fumbling around the inside. He smiled. Probably hiding her stash of pot, and accessories. Then, the door slowly opened. A girl, late teens, stood before him. She wore a dark tube top, and daisy dukes shorts. Her short blonde hair had been shaved on the left side, giving her tattoos on her neck, a visible image. Colored in they had a pentagram and several bright stars on it. She smiled at Billy, and studied his crotch for a moment. Billy shifted his feet nervously, at her gaze. "Can I help you, officer, she said dreamily. Her eyes were puffy, and he could smell the Marijuana on her. "Wow, he thought, I might get a contact high. He stepped back a few, She started, then said, "I'm Sweet Patti', she said, and you? "Detective Walker to you", he said, trying to be formal." "Well she said, you're cute for a cop". She rubbed her hands over her tube top, revealing her erect nipples. Billy swallowed hard, and then continued. "Have you seen anything unusual lately? He queried. The girl laughed, "All the time! "I mean really", he said, seriously. The girl regarded him for a moment, and then saw Annie, / Marie standing behind him. "Is that your sister? She asked cattily. "Why . . ." Annie/Marie growled at her, her eyes beginning to glow red hot. 'Enough! Billy said, "Answer my question". The girl stepped back, looking nervously at them. She breathed out, and then replied, "Some guy, a big bastard, snuck into your apartment! She continued, "He stayed maybe ten minutes then left". Billy had figured the gangster would pull something on them. "Thanks", Billy said, then turned to Annie/Marie. "I expected this, let's go in". Annie/Marie looked at him puzzled. He urged her to the door. The girl said, 'Let me know if you wanted something tasty", then licked her lips loudly, and slammed the door. Annie/Marie almost said something, but changed her mind, and entered the apartment with Billy. "What . . . she began, than Billy pressed his fingers to her lips. He shushed her, and then pointed to the bedroom. Annie/Marie wasn't sure what was going on, but she followed Billy into the bedroom. 'Here's what's happening, he said. He stepped to the shower, and turned it on full blast. He came back, and began to talk to her in a low voice. 'The gangster has a device to listen in on us". "It was planted while we were out." Annie/Marie nodded, listening carefully. "I have an informant who can help us". "We'll leave in a few to go see him". He continued, "How's your vision? 'It's becoming clearer now; I can almost see the place. "It's some kind of factory, but I don't know the exact place! Billy replied, "We will go talk to Sneaky Pete, my inside guy, and maybe find out. Billy turned off the shower, and they left. Armano seen them leave. "Want us to follow them? Johnny asked. Armano nodded, adding, "Unless you want to talk to the woman, who I suspect is some kind of witch! Johnny frowned, "*Come un ditto nel culo*" {Like a finger up my asshole}, he replied. Armano laughed out loud at Johnny. It was the first time in a while, his sense of humor had returned. They drove off, keeping a safe distance from the two detectives. Billy glanced in the mirror. "We're being followed, he pronounced to her. "Really" she said, turning around to look. "Ignore them", he said to her. 'O.k.", she said. 'They're just going to follow us". 'They won't learn anything from it, anyway", Billy concluded. Billy and Annie/Marie arrived at a seedy looking theater downtown. Trash was guarding it revengefully. Broken wine and beer bottles were adorning the sides of the building. The building itself had been poorly maintained. The roof looked beaten as if in a war zone. Several windows had been recently boarded up. The marquee dirty with dust, proclaimed "XXX movies her, 24-7". Admission only five dollars. "My god! Annie/Marie thought, what a dump! "How does this keep going like that", she asked Billy. "Who knows", he said to her, getting out. He continued, "Plenty of twisted minds around here! "Watch were you step", he added, stepping over some trash and broken bottles. Annie/Marie stepped carefully around the garbage, accidentally stepping on a broken bottle with a loud crunch under her leather boots. Damn glad I wore these she said, or I'd get some septic poison from all this crap. They stepped into the ill lit lobby. A swarthy looking man in his fifties stood there, and held out his hand to them. Billy flashed his shield at him. "Oh, shit! The man exclaimed, "Is this a bust". He fidgeted nervously with his hands. "Not this time", Billy said, putting his badge away. 'You seen Sneaky Pete", Billy asked. Yeah . . . Yeah ", the man replied. He continued, 'Second row near the front". 'He alone? Billy asked. The man was sweating a lot now. "That old whore Dorothy is down there with him. "Probably polishing his knob. His face turned a little red, seeing Annie/Marie studying him closely. "Why do they call him Sneaky Pete? She asked. Billy grinned, "He's a small time thief. Sneaks into people's homes, and steals their valuables, stereos, and TVs. "He's also known to be a serial masturbator", he finished, waiting for her reaction. She frowned a look of disgust. "Oh, lovely", she said, moving her hand up and down in an obscene gesture, letting her tongue hang out. Billy laughed, heartily. Annie returned with a grin. "Give me your flashlight! He demanded at the man. The man reached into the back pocket of his baggy khakis and handed it to Billy. Billy told her, "come on let's look for him. They stepped into the darkened theater. He could hear the moans coming out of the screen. A man and woman were engaged in oral sex Billy admired it for a moment, and then continued on down the aisles, the flashlight, illuminating the seats. Several business types here during their lunch hour, to get a quick fix. Two gay men towards the back, giggling. Billy couldn't see their hands, just as well, he thought! Down the rows they went, Annie/Marie catching the odor of stale urine, and something else foul, she refused to identify. The two came upon Billy. Dorothy's' head bobbing up and down in Pete's lap. Dorothy of what Billy could see had slowly gone downhill. Abscesses on both arms, from shooting up. Her once illustrious dark hair, matted in clumps, and very dirty. Billy sighed sadly. The streets suck the life out of you! Like some rampant vampire on the loose, it drained everything human right out of you. If the drugs don't kill you, the lifestyle will. Billy crept up to Dorothy, still going at it, oblivious to her surroundings. Billy gently tapped on her shoulder. Dorothy jerked up in surprise. "Ow! Pete said" you bit me". Billy grinned. Dorothy looked at Billy, smiling. "Hi, Billy, she said, smiling at him. Billy noticed most of her teeth gone, rotted away. Pete sat up, covering his groin. A grin spread out on his face. Then his face changed a different color, when he saw Billy there. "Oh, shit! He said, looking at Billy and Annie/Marie. "Am I busted? He asked, nervously. "Not this time, Petey", Billy stated. "We need some info", Billy continued, "Got a little money on you now? Asked Billy. Pete just nodded. "Where you get it, stealing? Pete looked at him, liked Billy had insulted him. "Legitimate job man, I swear" Pete stated. ""Doing what? Billy asked "I . . . I swore not to tell" Pete said, stuttering. "Want to go to jail for public indecency, Billy told him, raising his voice. 'Wasn't indecent ", Pete said definitely. "I can make it stick", commented Billy, producing a set if handcuffs from his belt. "Hold on a minute, boss", Pete said, and then zipped up his trousers. "What do you want to know? "The money! Billy demanded. "I got it on the square believe me", Pete began to explain. "I was crashed out at the doorway to the old steel factory. Billy nodded, urging him on. "Someone kicked me, waking me up. "There stood a man, maybe in his forties, looking down at me! 'I said what the hell you want". The man kicked me again. Then, he said "Want to make a few bucks, fool, he said. 'WH . . . what do you want me to do", he asked warily. Sirocco just smiled. "I need you guard this building. "I'll give you twenty now, and forty later when the job is done". 'What else? Pete asked. "Just open the door, and yell if someone comes creeping around". Sirocco handed Pete the twenty. "How do you know I won't just keep it, and take off? Pete asked. Sirocco gave him an evil grin, like Pete had never seen before. "Then I'll introduce you to my nasty friend". With that, he pointed his finger at something behind Pete. Pete smelled it first. A smoky smell, like brimstone, and the smell of rotted flesh punctuated the air. The hairs on Pete's neck stood up, as he slowly turned around, fear fluctuating in his face. Pete's eyes bulged out, like they were going to explode. He stared in horror! Their before him, stood something like a nightmare, a living, breathing monster! Pete shook in every part of his body. His legs trembling, almost on the verge of collapsing.

# Chapter Eleven

I t was the worse he ever saw, the smell of rotted flesh, engraved into his nostrils. It grinned at him, licking its lips over the razor sharp teeth. Pete stood there, transfixed. Then he heard Sirocco's voice behind him. "I think he gets the point, Bacalou! The thing smiled the most horrific smile Pete had ever seen, and then vanished into smoke. The smell still lingered on to Pete's nose. Pete trembling turned to face the man. "What is your name? Sirocco asked, nonchalantly. "P . . . P PETE ", I said to the man. Pete paused in his narrative, swallowing like he couldn't breathe. "And? Annie/Marie asked. "Just a minute", Pete said, the color in his face, returning to his natural, pasty face. "That's all, swear to god", he said, making the sign of the cross. "Give me the address! Billy demanded, pulling out a small notebook. Annie/ Marie produces a small pen and gave it to Billy. Pete mumbled, barely audible to Billy's ears. Billy writes it down, and then handed the pen back to her. Annie/Marie saw that Pete's pants were soiled with urine. Disgusted, she said, "What a little worm." She turned to Dorothy, who sat mesmerized at everything. "You leave! She commanded to Dorothy. Dorothy shook her head, and then jumped up in a hurry to leave. As she attempted to breeze past Annie/Marie, the woman grabbed her both arms, squeezing them tightly. Dorothy opened her eyes wide struggling. Annie/ Marie touched Dorothy's lips with a finger. "Shh! she said quietly to Dorothy. Dorothy relaxed, a look of peace came across her brow. Annie/Marie began mumbling to Dorothy, gripping her arms still tightly. A rush of air filled the room. The smell of jasmine, and sweet honey erupted, filling the very air around everyone. Billy and Pete inhaled the smell into their lungs. It gave them a sense of peace, well being. Annie/ Marie continued chanting. "Be gone you evil poison! She shouted into Dorothy's face. Dorothy's body began to shiver and shake uncontrollably. Tears filled her eyes, flooding her cheap tattered orange t-shirt. Then she stopped, stood straight into Annie/Maries eyes. Looking amazed, she gazed down on her arms. They were clean, no more abscesses or scaring from the dirty needles was there! She burst into laughter of joy! She touched her hair, it was shiny and clean, as it was before her descent into hell! "Oh, thank you", she said, and kissed Annie/Marie on the cheek. "Go and do no more harm to yourself! Annie/Marie commanded her. "Go home to your family, who loves you, and will forgive you! "Go now! Annie /Marie smiled at her. What sounded like a holler of joy and thankfulness escaped from Dorothy's lips, as she ran full blast from the theater Billy and Pete looked at her, amazement on their faces. Billy spoke first. "Damn . . . Billy began, "I've seen it all! Annie/Marie looked at him. "A choice for a better life. "It's all up to her now what she does with it. Billy looked at Pete. Annie/Marie looked at Pete; a frown appeared upon her face. "His path leads somewhere else", She stated. Billy looked at her. Pete just smirked. "So long perv", Billy said, nodding to Annie/Marie. They left Pete sitting there, a scowl crossing his face. Fuck them! He thought, and returned to watching the skin flick. Armano gazed at the two leaving. "Wonder what that was about? Asked Johnny to his boss. Maybe a lead", Armano replied. "Let's wait till their gone, and go in to find out". Johnny nodded, and sat back in his seat, calmly waiting. Pete continued watching the movie. His hand reaching into his pants. Goddamn Dorothy didn't finish! And those asshole cops interrupted them. Pete continued concentrating on his crotch. Then he smelled it! The rotted smell he had smelt before. The air filled his nostrils with the brimstone smell. Oh shit! Pete thought, I got to get out! He jumped up, attempting to zip up his trousers. The figure of Bacalou appeared before him. "Hey, little man let me help you with that! He growled. Pete felt his bowels beginning to loosen up. Bacalou, his long claws descended, grabbing Pete's' genitals. Pete opened his mouth to scream. Too late! Bacalou began ripping off Pete's genitals. Pete moaned in agony. Blood poured out from his groin, a spray that decorated the seats in front of him. In shock, Pete looked down at his missing genitals. Horrified, his bowels unloaded in his pants. Tears filled his eyes, as Bacalou tore Pete's body apart, his head landing at Bacalou' s feet. His eyes blinked twice, and then just went blank. Bacalou growled, now I eat your soul! He proceeded to ingest Pete's brain, licking his lips. 'Yummy! He laughed, and vanished. The two gay guys in the back, jumped up, rearranging their trousers, and ran like the wind out. Two business men vomited up on the floor, got up, and went screaming out the door. The attendant seeing every one panicking rushed down to the darkened theater. He then saw what was left of Pete scattering all over the seats. He turned a pale green in his face. And rushed out the theater to call 911. Armano and his two bodyguards observed the men rushing out yelling and running down the streets. '"What the fuck . . . Armano began, then got out of the vehicle. The two Johnny, and the other got out also, the three headed towards the theater door. The two bodyguards grabbed their weapons out, and ran in front of their boss. Opened the door carefully, they stepped in, the two bodyguards, aiming their weapons around. All was quiet! Then Johnny went to open the doors to where the seats were. As he stood inside, the sickly smell of death assailed him. "Sweet mother of god! Johnny muttered, crossing himself. 'In here! He yelled to the others. They all gathered at the aisles of seats, and slowly moved forward down them. They stopped, coming across what use to be Pete. His body parts scattered around the plush theater seats, giving it a bizarre effect. The movie was still playing, its screen illuminating occasionally the already horrific scene. "Jesus Christ! Armano uttered. He stepped forward for a closer look. 'Wonder who he pissed off"< Johnny commented, staying clear of the body parts. The worse was the skull, half eaten away. Its eyes blank but seem to be staring at Armano. Then its eyes fluttered, and the gnawed at mouth opened up. A voice like that, echoed into their ears. The sound of a death rattle, emerging through it. "Stay and watch the movie boys, it's a killer! Then the mouth closed, the skull rotated, flying up in the air. "Fuck! Fuck! Johnny said, aiming at the skull with his gun. The skull careened around the seats, diving at them, cackling. Johnny fired three shots, shattering what was left of the skull, into pieces! Oh, shit! Came the last sound from the skull, as it fell into pieces at their feet. "Let's go! Armano shouted at the two, "Away from this evil place! The three hurried out the door, getting into the vehicle, and speeding off. They could hear the sounds of police cars near. Armano shook his head. "What the hell had he got into? He was still resolved to find his daughter no matter what, even if it cost him his life. Armano sat there thinking grimly about what may be coming. Billy and Annie/ Marie were back at the apartment, looking at a map of the county. Billy pointed at a spot on the map. "I know this area, well". He continued, "In the north end of town. Once a thriving steel production was there, now just rusting away". "What happened? She asked, leaning over his shoulder to get a better look." Production was low, as the Chinese competition was better priced. "We sold out, for the cheaper deal! One thousand people lost their jobs, and the plant closed down. "What happened to Yankee ingenuity? She asked. People got lazy. They looked for the easy way out. He continued, "It's sad the way the economy runs". "So much for the American dream", she said, shaking her head. "You got it! Land of the free, my ass! Annie/Marie shook her head again. "I'll be glad to go back, this country is going to ruin. "Can't say I blame you", Billy commented sadly. "Now to go out and check this place out", she said. Billy gathered up the map, and they left. Armano had returned with his two, watching the pair leave. "Follow them? Johnny turned around and asked his boss, sitting quietly in the back seat. Armano nodded, and then said, "Not to close". Johnny nodded, and said something to the driver. They followed the two, back about five car links. They all continued down the road, turning left on Western, and continued out to a stretch of unpaved road. They followed it for three miles, and then came to a heavily armed area of weeds, brownish looking sick grass, and dead bushes. Beyond that was the old factory, standing out of all of it, like some rusty giant overlooking its land? Billy and Annie/Marie stared at the old factory. Remnants of an old productive past. "We should get closer", she advised Billy. Billy and her got out of the car, and continued to wade through the deep brush, trying to be quiet. As they crept along, they encountered thistles and expansive overgrowth of bushes along the way. Billy cursed in a low voice, as he caught some prickly thistles in his jacket. They crept along, almost one hundred yards from the factory. He heard Annie/Maria cried out'Damn I stepped in something". She shook her right boot. Billy smiled, "Looks like dog shit to me! "Uh . . . she mumbled. Billy held his finger to his lips, in a be quiet manner. She gave him a dirty look, but squatted down to hide herself better. They looked up at the entrance to the factory. There it sat, guarding the entrance. Billy and Annie/Marie stared at it. They looked at each other. "Oh, shit! Annie/Marie said in a low tone. "What is that! Billy exclaimed, looking at the grey scaly image in their eyes." Bacalou! Annie/Marie pronounced in a low tone of voice. Billy stared at it again. "Don't make it handsome where it comes from,' he said gritting his teeth. Annie smiled, "He is the most malevolent god of voodoo", she replied. She continued, "We have to wait for the blood moon". "That way it will be preoccupied with the man and his ritual. Billy nodded. The thing lifted its head, sniffing in the air.'Oh, oh, I think it smells us! Billy told her. Annie/Marie waved her hands in the air several times, speaking an ancient tongue, not like Haitian. Billy felt a bubble surrounded him and her. "Ancient Sumerian, to protect us", she said through the bubble, its shape barely visible. "Let's go", Billy whispered. They took off, moving quickly, trying to be quiet as possible. Armano, parked a block away, saw them moving fast through the brush. "What should we do? Asked Johnny, looking at his boss. "Whatever it is, it scared the crap out of them", he replied. "Let's just follow them. He finished," Whatever scared them, I don't want to know." Johnny nodded, and waited for the two could get to the car. The two detectives took off, spinning gravel as they left. Armano's driver pulled away, moving at a slow clip, keeping at a distance from the two. Armano leaned back in his seat, slipping into deep thought.

Billy and Annie/Marie arrived back at the apartment. They went up the stairs, Billy shaken by what he saw. The next door window curtain opened slightly, than closed quickly. Billy didn't even catch a glance of the girl, but the music was turned down. Billy knew that the girl had seen them. The two entered the apartment and sat down on the couch. Billy looked at Annie/Marie, and said, "What now? She crossed her legs, and said, "When the blood moon rises tomorrow night, we will make our move. ""Things will get chaotic then. But with Dumballah's help, we will overcome all". Billy said, "If you don't mind, I'll be carrying my firearm too". Annie/ Marie smiled, "I also, but it only pertains to the mortal". Billy nodded, and got up to make some coffee. Annie/Marie closed her eyes, humming in her meditations. Billy looked, and then smiled, making his coffee; he sat down at the table, sorting though his mind for a plan to work. Armano was parked outside Billy's apartment, listening in to the bug Johnny had planted. "Nothing going on yet, till tomorrow night, He said. "Drive us home for now". The driver nodded. Johnny sat back in the passenger seat. What had he gotten himself into? He was indebted to his boss, but he thought Armano was losing it. Johnny shook his head. If worse went to bad, he was going to bail. Fuck all this mumbo jumbo shit! Other gangsters he could deal with. But this shit wasn't jiving in his brain. Johnny shook his head again. We'll see what happens! He thought to himself. The three men rode back to Armano's house in silence. Sirocco grinned pleased with himself. The body of the naked Haitian girl lay on the table, motionless, but not for long. Son his beloved would be back. If he timed it right, he could rid himself Of Bacalou, the voodoo child, and Erzule all at the same time. Little did he know, that part of the evil one, was steadily taking control of him. A flash of pain, shattered his thoughts. Probing, seeking his mind. Sirocco shook his head, trying to clear it. "W 'what . . . he started. Thoughts of another, raced through his mind." Do not do this! The voice said. "Leave your wife in peace. Bacalou will consume you, and leave the world in darkness." But Sirocco was determined. He shouted out loud, "Get out of me! He hollered. Bacalou stepped in from outside. He saw that Sirocco had a look of distress on his face! Bacalou approached him, and then grasped the Bokar's head gently in his claws. He felt the invading thoughts running constantly through Sirocco and him! Bacalou growled, then started chanting in some ancient tongue, "Depart from him, witch, or I will seek you out and destroy your very being! The thoughts fluttered in Sirocco's mind, then vanished. Sirocco bent over the table that held the body, and said, "Damn! "What was that! Bacalou replied, releasing the bokar's head. "An invasion from some witch, trying to control you". She would try to stop you from completed the ritual". "Why? Sirocco asked, trembling. Bacalou stated in a booming voice, "She wants the world to stay the same, and you would lose your beloved". She is only concerned with what she wants and nobody else". Sirocco gathered himself together. "Well fuck her! He exclaimed. "Excellent idea", Bacalou laughed, and then I'll eat her soul". His claws clapped together, gleefully. Sirocco looked in disgust, and then returned to examining the naked girl, making sure everything was ready for the blood moon. Erzule watched with fascination, as he continued his examination. She spoke quietly to Angelica, who waited impatiently to return. "How soon, mama? She asked a whisper to Erzule's mind. "Soon my child, we will both have our vengeance! Erzule could feel Angelica's voice shivering. "Be still child, for one more night, and we will be freed. ' Angelica then quieted down, waiting! Erzule smiled. Sirocco looked up at Erzule, who was smiling wide. "Wonder what the hell she looks so so happy about? He asked himself. Then he merely shrugged, opening up his grimoire, his book of spells, preparing for tomorrow night. Bacalou sat in silent thought, preparing his part in the upcoming ritual. All was still for right now;

# Chapter Twelve

Armano was reviewing his options. What to do next? He needed to set up a base of operations near the two detectives place. Then when the time was right, he would follow them back to the factory. Armano smiled anxiously. Soon he would get his sweet Angelica back, and to hell with all this black magic. He would pick up the pieces after they were done with that, and grab his daughter! He hoped it would all come together, but one never knows what could happen. He must plan for any divergence that occurs. He decided to rest for a while. The lack of sleep was making him clouded in his brain. He wanted to be perfectly clear, when the moment happens. He lapsed into a deep sleep. Johnny and the other guy, Gino posted themselves at the door of their boss. Sirocco had come up with a diversion to keep the cops busy. He laughed gleefully at his plan. It's going to be a hot time in the old town tonight! The voodoo child looked at him puzzled. Whatever it was, she knew it was going to be disastrous for someone or others. She mumbled a little. She strained, using what little power she could summon up. She heard the chains buckle a little. But it wasn't enough. She sighed, and then looked at Sirocco. He was busy reading his spell book again. He obviously hadn't heard her. The sweat from her exertions dripped down on her. Her body was completely nude. She felt ashamed for Angelica, who was also suffering in her shame, at her nakedness. "Soon! Tomorrow, Erzule soothed Angelica. She felt Angelica relaxing, and rested. Sirocco pulled out a map of the city. There it was he pointed at the courthouse. A good spot for an explosion. The civic center with their sanctimonious assholes was another. He could place the explosives at the courthouse, under the benches. The civic center that had a town hall meeting would be easy. He would mingle in the crowd till he got close to the podium. He could slip the explosives under the stage. There was an open space where the PA system was located. That would be perfect! Sirocco rubbed his hands together, smiling at the thought. The mayor would be there. A great opening ceremony for the mayor, Bob Hersey, just newly elected! Sirocco smiled. A great experience for years to come. Sirocco pulled out the building plans and began study them. He hummed a little tune, while he continued. Bacalou grinned, knowing what Sirocco was planning. Bacalou continued probing into the Bokar's mind. McCarthy sat at his desk, holding his head. The chief had just read him the riot act. Marlon sat at his computer, looking over the hate mail. He had almost pinpointed the IP adress of the sender. "I think I found them", Marlon commented to his boss. "Where? McCarthy asked, looking up. "I don't think you'll like it", Marlon quipped, "Well who the hell is it! He bellowed at Marlon. Marlon shrunk back in his seat. He began to stutter, "It . . . it's your ex-wife, Glenda! McCarthy slammed his fist on the table. "That bitch! Divorced, and still after my balls! He turned around, and called two uniforms into his office. "Go pick this woman up, and bring her in", he commanded the two. The older cop, on the force for twenty years, named Gregg, looked at the address his boss had handing him. Gregg took off his cap, and scratched his balding grey head. "Are you sure boss? he asked. Gregg recognized the ex-wife's name. Hell, he had met her before at one of the police barbecues' yearly event. After meeting her Gregg reflected, she was pretty well high strung, too nervous to be a cop's wife. The marriage lasted five years, along with numerous verbal threats, and she'd punched him in the face once. Gregg's conclusion . . . That woman definitely had issues. "Damn right, McCarthy said, "She is the one sending the hate mail! He pounded his fist on his desk, his face glowing bright red. "Jesus", Gregg muttered," O.K., let's go", he said to his partner Jamie Osaki. Gregg left with his partner in a patrol car, heading to Glenda's. Gregg filed in the situation to his partner. Jamie was Japanese, one of the few on the force, still a rookie; he enjoyed working with his dour and sometimes funny trainer. They arrived at the location. Getting out, Gregg told him, "Let me handle this, I know her", he said to his partner. A nice two story brick house, with a lush garden along side of it. Gregg knocked on the door. Glenda sitting on the couch heard the knock. At first, she ignored it. Someone was filling her thoughts with messages. The image of the man reminded her of some movie star, but she couldn't remember the name. "Do what I say", Bacalou told her, "And I'll take good care of you, forever! He spoke in a whisper, telling her what to-do. She nodded her head, and smiled. She got up to answer the door, in tight jeans shorts, and a t-shirt. Her mousy blonde hair set up in curlers. She answered the door, where the two cops stood. One was an older cop, she recognized. The other, an oriental, young in his twenties, stood looking nervously. She smiled at them. "Gregg isn't it", she said to the older one. "Yes, maam", Gregg replied, taking off his hat. Glenda remembered he was always polite to her in the past. "I know why you're here", she said to Gregg, then looked at Jamie. "Who's the jap?, she asked frowning. "Be polite now, Glenda, he's my partner". Smiling again, she said apologetically "Sorry". "You need to come with us to the station", Gregg said, steeling himself for the verbal abuse she was so fond off. Nothing! She smiled, and said, "I need to get my shoes". Gregg sighed in relief, "Ok., but leave the door open. The two officers stepped inside. "I'll be just a minute", She smiled again at them, going into her bedroom. She grabbed her open toed shoes that strapped around her ankles. She secured them, then looking around to see if she was being watched. She reached under her mattress retrieving an eight inch butcher's knife, and stuffed it down her shorts. She looked to see if it showed. Her long t-shirt covered her to her thighs. Nothing could be seen, She exited the bedroom slowly, trying not to feel the blade there, against her crouch. Hope nothing gets cut down there! She exited with the two officers to their patrol car. Jamie looked at his partner. "Should we search her? He asked. 'Can't replied, Gregg. "Not without a female officer present." "You don't have anything dangerous in your shorts do you? Glenda gave him her sexiest smile. "Just my pussy". Greggs face blushed, while Jamie leered at her. "Never mind, Gregg said, still blushing, then instructed her to get in the back seat of the patrol car. She sat down, still smiling. "We going to cuff her?, Jamie asked cautiously. "it's not necessary, I'll cooperate. ". "it's ok. She's being cooperative enough", Gregg said to his partner. As they drove off, she said, "I forgot my bra, and panties", She looked at the two pretending to be embarrassed. "We're professionals, don't worry. Jamie turned his head a little, observing her erect nipples protruding from her flimsy t-shirt. She gave him a grin, licked her lips, and rubbed her nipples. Jamie stared, and Gregg noticed it as he was driving. "Ignore her", Gregg said, then said to Glenda, "Behave yourself".

Glenda stopped rubbing her breasts, and said, "sorry you are a gentleman". She lapsed into quiet reflection, The voice whispering suggestions in her mind. They arrived at the station without incident. The two officers escorted her to the front desk. The duty sergeant, a heavy set man in his fifties, and bald, his head glistening sweat on it. "What have we got here?, he asked Horsley, wiping sweat off his head. "Going into interrogation for questioning. Glenda winked, then lifted her t-shirt a little to reveal one of her breasts. It was a quick flash, the two officers hadn't even registered to it. The duty sergeant saw it briefly. He grinned. Then he pressed a button, beneath his desk, a buzzer sounded, and the two officers with Glenda in the front, strode in to the main office. Glenda turned her head to the duty sergeant as they entered, saying, "You ought to give up that three beer lunches". The desk sergeant turned red in the face, muttered something to himself, and then started looking over some arrest reports on his desk. As the door closed behind him, Gregg just shrugged, looking at his partner. "I always knew he tossed off a few at lunch, He's do for retirement in seven days". Jamie just looked at him, Jamie nodded his head.. That's the way things worked here! Best to go along with the program. ' Gregg said again, "I always told him to drink Vodka instead of beer, It smells less". Stress of the job, I guess, Jamie thought. The two escorted Glenda to where McCarthy sat. A grim look on his face as he stared at Glenda. Even in her forties, she still was looking good. She smiled at him, then spat in his direction, it landing on his desk. McCarthy jumped back, like a bullet was aimed at him. "Hi asshole, she grinned, Want to fuck me! The two officers were shocked looking perplexed. McCarthy started to get up. Glenda peeled off her clothes, grasping the deadly blade in her hand, shining brightly in the dim office. Standing naked, her legs apart, McCarthy got a view of her bush, which caused him to be distracted. Jamie jumped forward as she started to swing the blade around at his boss. He grasped her around the waist, pulling her away. They both slipped on the carpet, and fell, with Glenda riding on top. She kissed the startled Jamie, then holding the blade tightly, in her hand, plunged it deeply into his groin. Blood spurted, as Jamie released her, screaming "Oh my nuts! My nuts! He reached down to try and slow the flood of blood spreading across his groin. McCarthy was transfixed in horror. Still his training kicked in. He went for his weapon. Gregg came around out of a trance, and stepped forward towards Glenda. She slashed at him with the knife, missing his chest by inches. Gregg stepped back, and went for his weapon. At that time, the heavy set desk sergeant came fumbling through, having heard the commotion. He saw the oriental cop lying in a pool of blood, crying out. Gregg had pulled his weapon, and cocked his thirty eight. He paused for a moment. The crazed woman was screaming at the boss, and gnashing her teeth. She looked at the boss, her knife at her side. "You'll die assholes, all of you, when the blood moon rises! She gripped the knife tightly, swinging the knife dangerously in an arc. The old sergeant withdrew his colt 45, and fired at her. The bullet struck her in the back of her neck. She paused for a moment, and blinked, not realizing she had been shot. Then she collapsed across McCarthy's desk, blood splattering all over his paperwork. "Oh, my god! The old desk sergeant said. He grabbed his chest, then collapsed on the floor. A fatal heart attack, due to inactivity, and one too many beers. Only seven days left, was his last thought, as the darkness surrounded him. McCarthy stood in horror at the scene. Gregg shook his head, and put his pistol back in his holster. "Godamn, he said, I've never seen shit like this before". He stepped towards the naked body. All her bodily fluids had erupted on the bosses' desk. McCarthy stood in a trance, his weapon still drawn. He snapped out of it, as Gregg approached him. "I need you to get it together, boss. "We've got a hell of a mess to straighten out! McCarthy nodded, then went to his ex wife's body, slowly, and checked her pulse. Nothing! She was gone. He was still in shock of what happened. Gregg spoke up, then McCarthy climbed down to reality. "We need an ambulance for Jamie, and I think the desk sergeant had dropped dead from a heart attack". McCarthy took in the situation. Help Jamie till the ambulance arrives'. "I'll call the coroner, and the ambulance myself! McCarthy grabbed his phone, speaking fast into it, giving directions. Other offices from down the hall had rushed in. "What the fuck! One stated, almost tripping over the body of the desk sergeant. Bent over one of them checked the dead man's pulse. "Serge is gone", he pronounced grimly. Gregg just nodded. He was holding Jamie in his arms. Poor kid! He thought.

Jamie gripped Gregg's arm tight. "Don't let them take off my balls", he moaned, then gave Gregg a weak smile. The last thing he heard before passing out, was the roaring sound of the ambulance sirens, blaring its morose warning. McCarthy sat down hard in his chair, staring at his dead wife's body, draped casually across his desk. Gregg looked up, as Marlon, late from lunch came busting through the door. "Sorry boss traffic was . . . he stopped, seeing the chaotic scene, the oriental cop on the floor, bleeding to death, a dead woman sprawled across his bosses' desk. Marlon stopped in mid stride, stood still; his legs begin to wobble, and then vomited. What was left of his lunch splattered the floor, some of it ending up on the closer officers' shoes. "Shit! the officer yelled. He turned to admonish Marlon. Marlon eyes rolled upward, exposing only the whites. Then he collapsed in a heap on the floor by the offer's feet. "Just dandy! Exclaimed McCarthy, getting up, to check on Marlon. The ambulance arrived with the gurney, the younger one of the two exclaimed "Jesus Christ! The older one shook his head. He had seen a lot, but this takes the cake, by god! McCarthy pointed to the wounded cop, Jamie who lay on the floor, clutching his crotch. The two attendants picked him up carefully, and hauled him out the door quickly. They could hear him moaning and crying all the way out. Then the coroner arrived, a new guy, replacing Bud. Dugan had quit, and moved out of the state. "Who are you? McCarthy asked suspiciously. "Jake Holden, the new coroner, just arrived today". He went to shake McCarthy's hand, and then realized he had his latex gloves on. He withdrew his hand, and then said, 'Sorry about that, what have we got here? "A mentally ill woman, who came in, and attacked us! Gregg spoke up." "Talk about P.M.S. ", Jake said, off hand. McCarthy frowned at him. "Just do your Job! He said loudly to Jake. Something about the coroner bothered him. Some strange smell emanated from him he couldn't quite identify. Jake merely shrugged, went to his coroner's van, and retrieved a steel gurney to remove the body. He placed it close to the desk as he could. "Well, here comes the really icky part. He motioned to McCarthy and Gregg to help. They leaned over the desk to help with the removal. The blood pool had gathered up under her.

As they pulled, the body made a sticky sound, like peeling away Velcro. McCarthy felt sick to his stomach; the gorge began to gather up from his stomach, burning his throat. He forced the gorge down, coughing and hacking. Gregg looked at him, concerned. "I'm all right, let's get this done". They maneuvered the body squarely onto the gurney. "I can get it from here out" Jake said, pushing the gurney out the door. Several officers stepped aside to let him out. "Christ! McCarthy thought, shits going to hit the fan. Gregg placed his hand on his bosses' shoulder in sympathy. Reluctantly, he grabbed the phone, and dialed the chief. The chief answered it, not in the best of moods. Here it goes, thought, McCarthy, waiting for the gallows to fall. Jake the coroner drove off, heading in the opposite direction of the morgue. He hummed some unknown tune as he drove. Traveling to a heavy wooded area of the north end, he pulled over. Crawling to the back of the vehicle, He leaned over Glenda. He slapped her face twice. Then his tongue forked, and slobbering moved slowly down her throat. He paused, looking for her soul. He pulled out, recovering a plasma object, about the size of a roll of nickels. He pressed it to his lips, and swallowed it. "I have your soul now! He growled, his voice changing into Bacalou, grated sound. He grinned, and then slapped the dead woman hard across the face. "Rise up bitch; you are mine now to do what I wish! Glenda opened her eyes, sat up, and blinked at Jake/, Bacalou. He smiled at her. Rubbing his hands together, He growled, "Now the fun begins! Glenda nodded a blank look on her face. "Come up front with me! He commanded her. Naked, and some of her grey matter protruding from her head, she climbed over the seat. She sat staring ahead, and then placed her hand on his thigh. Bacalou grinned, and then observed her leaking "Skull. There. "We'll have to fix that now that your mine! He drove off gleefully humming the same unknown tune. This will surprise a lot of those mortals. Annie was aroused out of her trance, as the phone rang. "Sure you want to answer? Billy asked her, getting up from the kitchen table. "Guess I will" she replied, "It could be important". Billy nodded, probably not really wanting to know. "Hello", she answered in a calm voice. Billy could hear McCarthy's voice, strained and excitable from where he stood. Annie's eyes grew large as he talked. He heard McCarthy mumble something low, and then Annie hung up the phone. Her face was pale, and her lips trembled a bit. "What is it? Billy asked, moving closer to her. "ALL hell has broken out at the station, I'll tell you on the way! Billy grabbed his keys off the coffee table, and the two headed out the door to the car. Annie filled Billy in on the incident. Billy stared in disbelief as Annie finished. He shook his head. "When will this end", He said, trying to concentrate on the road. Annie replied, when the blood moon rises high, near midnight. "Billy drove on deep in his thoughts. They arrived, chaos residing all around them. CSI was there. Many police officers were milling around, pacing nervously. "What the hell is this? Billy exclaimed to one the officers, puffing hard on a cigarette. He looked at Billy, sadly. "Goddamn mess," he stated, stubbing out his cigarette. The two detectives just nodded, and stepped inside. The place was full of uniforms, and The CSI team. Billy and Annie stepped around the crowd, seeing McCarthy, and a uniform, who Billy recalled as Gregg. "Hey boss", Billy greeted the man, who was running fingers through his hair, relentlessly. McCarthy responded, "A hell of a mess! Glenda was the one sending the hate mail! She came in here, stripped naked, and had a butcher knife, stabbing Jamie, then the old desk sergeant shot her, and had a heart attack, fatal, and died on the floor. He pointed to the floor where the old guy lay, waiting for the coroner to return. Someone out of respect had found a blanket, covering him up. McCarthy grew angry. "When the hell is he coming back? McCarthy stepped over to his phone, and dialed it. Waiting for the answer, he commented "He's been gone for at least ninety minutes. Then said, "Why didn't he take both of them". A female voice answered. McCarthy explained the situation to her. "Sorry officer, we sent a coroner from Redlands, he should be there shortly". "I thought Jake Holden was the coroner? He asked. The female voice dropped to a lower level. "Jake? Jake? She resounded. "He was a coroner here ten years ago. He died in a tragic car wreck. She broke down, and cried. "We were engaged", she said though the crying. "What kind of sick joke is this? McCarthy responded, "I'm sorry, someone is impersonating him came here. She hung the phone line up, and McCarthy turned towards Annie, now secretly Marie Laveau, and Billy. His face was beyond pale, and looked like death. "What is it? Annie/Marie asked, stepping closer to him. His voice wavered a little. "I think we've been visited by a ghost! Annie/Marie smelled the air, her nostrils flaring widely. She stopped, and shook her head. "Evil . . . Bacalou was here! McCarthy looked at her, "Who the hell is he? Annie/Marie sighed, and then said, "The one of two who caused all this". She spread her hands out at the scene. "Voodoo, black magic shit? He asked her. She merely nodded her head. "Well . . . he began, and then paused; He pulled out a handkerchief, wiping his brow. "I I . . . Believe it now! "How the hell am I going to explain this with the chief"? Billy thought for a moment, the suggested, "Tell him it's a devil cult doing this. Explain to him we're going to raid them tomorrow night, and clear this up". "It just might work, I hope", his boss stated. "I'll give him a call". McCarthy returned to the office. Billy looked at Marlon, who sat in his chair, in a half faint. He stepped over to where he sat Marlon's eyes half open. He opened them all the way, looking at Billy. Annie/Marie leaned over Billy's shoulder.

"Who's the fuckboy? She asked. Marlon looked at her in surprise. "Why is she saying that? He asked. "Never mind, Billy said, she's having a bad day". Billy smiled at Marlon. "Go home Marlon, and get some rest ", Billy told him, looking sympathetically. "What about the boss? Marlon asked. "He's too busy right now, go ahead", Billy urged him. Marlon moaned a little, and then got out. "I'm going go over to Frank's place and stay there today. Then Marlon smiled. Frank was who he is dating now, a fashion photographer for Vogue. Would be glad to see him. Marlon grabbed his man purse from under his desk, and left. "What? Asked Annie/Marie. "He knows you well. Just pretend you know him". She shrugged her shoulders, and then said, "Ok", I get it". Billy and Annie/Marie left to return to their apartment. Billy had many more questions for her.

# Chapter Thirteen

Bacalou arrived at the factory with Glenda in tow. As they came through the door, Sirocco looked at the two. His face became hot with anger. "What the hell is this? He demanded. Bacalou gave a growl, and then said, his voice booming, shaking the walls. Sirocco's face turned from anger to fear. He trembled. Bacalou continued, stepping forward towards the man. "I rule here", he said," "The woman stays, I have plans for her that will help us, and me especially", he gave him an evil grin, licking his lips, and squeezing one of her breasts. Sirocco felt sick in his stomach, but just nodded, and returned to his spellbook ignoring them. Bacalou grinned, and took her into the old supervisor's office. He could hear their violent love making going on. Sirocco felt disgusted. Getting rid of Bacalou wouldn't be that easy. He frowned. Armano got up, got dressed, and called on Johnny, and the other guard, Gino. "Let's go, we're going to stake out those two detectives, when they leave! He said to them. They left the house, an Armano hoping his plan will work. Soon, he would get his Angelica back! They arrived and parked across the street from the two detectives. "Johnny asked, "How long do we wait? Armano answered, "S something about the blood moon, I heard, until then we need a base of operations." Johnny nodded, looking around. He smelled . . . Pizza! Pepperoni and sausage! His stomach growled. He hadn't eaten in a while. He turned to his boss. "How about that pizzeria". Armano replied "Good ", he said, "I've got to take a dump, and we'll get something to eat". Armano felt like his stomach had had its throat cut. They all drove up to the pizzeria, and parked. Getting out, Armano glanced at the sign in the window. Goldie's' Pizza, free delivery. One owner shop. Then Armano looked at the hours on it. Ten a.m. to nine p. m. probably only a few employees and the owner. This will maybe make it easier to take control of it. The three entered the shop. a little chime on the door announced them. "Johnny", Armano said, gets us something to eat; I have to take a dump'. Johnny nodded and stepped up to the counter. The woman at the counter, brushed her hands on her checkered apron, and greeted him. She looked to be in her late thirties, her long blonde hair tied up in a bun, regarded Johnny. She wore a white uniform blouse, the two buttons of it, unbuttoned revealing she had ample breasts. Armano stepped out of the restroom, and stepped up to the counter with Johnny and Gino. Armano gazed at her breasts, slightly peaking out of her uniform. She smiled at Armano. A nice looking man in a three piece suit. a dark charcoal in color. "Can I help you? She asked, looking at him. "You bet", Armano put his best charming smile at her. He gave her a wink. "I'd like two pepperoni and sausage pizzas and you", He said. The blonde smiled even more. "My name is Goldie". 'Well . . . Goldie", he began, and then whispered in her ear, her smile got even wider across her face. Armano reached into his pocket, and handed her what looked like several one hundred dollar bills. She blushed, and then looked around to see if her cook was looking. She stuffed the money into her pants uniform pocket. Armano nodded to her, and then pointed to the restroom. "O.K.", she said quietly. She turned to the cook, and said, "Slow day, take off". The cook sweating, in the back looked at her puzzled. He looked at the three standing at the counter. "Its o.k. Mike, she told him. She handed him one of the bills, putting it into his greasy hand. He just nodded, took off his apron, then left, thinking, what the fuck, no big deal. The hundred dollar bill equaled more than two days pay to him. Maybe I'll head over to Jelly's bar to toss off a few. "Me first, then make our pizzas ", Armano said. He motioned the two men, to set a table near the window. They could have a clear view of Billy's place. Goldie took her apron off, stepped out from behind the counter, and followed Armano into the men's restroom. Johnny got up from the table, and turned the open sign around to closed. Johnny turned to Gino. "Guess the boss needs some stress relief. He continued, "it'll be god for him'. Gino just lit a cigarette, and stared out the window. Johnny frowned at him. He didn't smoke. Bad for the lungs. He moved over to another table, and sat down. Gino just looked at him, smiling, and continued to smoke. The two bodyguards could hear their boss and the blonde, banging in the restroom, loudly. The two body guards sat silently, looking out the window. Annie/Marie pulled out a red kerchief, which held the magic of protection in it. "This is yours", she handed to Billy, who accepted it warily. "It smells", he he commented, wrinkling his nose. "It's not made to be a pleasant aroma, but to ward off evil", she replied to him. "Well shit! Billy said to her, that smell could make a dead man puke! She laughed at him, and then turned to Billy's cd player. She looked at it, scrutinizing the machine carefully. Billy started to show her how it works. She held her hand up, Slowing Billy's help to a standstill. She reached down next to the player, grabbed a disc, opened the player up, and inserted the disc. She smiled as it began to play. "Marie Laveau, voodoo, I put a spell on you". She began to turn in circles, doing a primitive dance. Billy watched her fascinated at her smooth rhythmic movements. "Come dance with me, Blanc", she urged, her hands open to invitation. Billy hesitated. "It's only a dance, honey. I haven't done this in a while. "Billy shyly approached her, then took her hands. "Feel it in your soul", she said desperately. Billy thought he wasn't that great at dancing, but they moved together, almost as one. Billy felt exhilarated, as they moved faster. Annie/Marie starting to perspire a little. Then the song was over. Emotions filled Billy's mind. She kissed him gently on the cheek. Billy began to feel aroused, and then shut it down. This was Annie's body, but not her mind. Billy stumbled away, mumbling. She smiled widely at him. "Thank you", she said, I feel much better now. It will give me a better positive aura for tomorrow night. "Billy just smiled sideways at her, and then sat down at the table, looking straight ahead at the bare wall. She glided over to him, and put a hand on his shoulder. 'it's ok, Blanc, this will soon is over, and I'll return Annie to you. No tricks! She rubbed his shoulders a little. She could feel his tenseness. Then he relaxed. He put his head down on the table, and lapsed into a snooze. She quietly tip toed into the bedroom. She began to chant softly. "**Dumballah,** come to me in secret! ""Come to me, now, at your pleasure. "A puff of smoke appeared above her head. It slowly twisted, forming into shape. He appeared, looking like a Rasfarian, with long dark dreadlocks, hanging down from his head. Annie/Marie looked surprised. "How do you like it? He asked her, A great disguise, huh? She blinked her eyes at him. He stood at normal stature, only about six feet tall. She smiled, and then nodded to him. "Does he know the price to pay, after all of this? he said quietly, referring to Billy, still snoozing at the table. "No! she replied to him, But he would do anything to save her". Dumballah thought this over. He shrugged his shoulders. "This is up to the greater powers than I, so it was decided, even if I objected, knowing I couldn't! She nodded her head at him. Then it's decided, fate intervenes". He nodded solemnly. "Call to me when the blood moon rises, high in the heavens. ". "Yes ", she replied," karma and fate will surpass it all". He vanished quietly, a puff of smoke, dissipating in the air. Annie / Marie sighed, let out a breath, and returned to the front room. If it goes well, there will be later sadness and mourning. Success, the word sat like a curse, as she wished to spit it out of her thoughts. She went over to Billy, and woke him up. 'Huh, huh? He asked, lifting his head up wearily. "How long did I nap? "Why don't you stretch out on the bed for a while, she said. He looked up at her. "I won't bother you. I need to gather all my spells together for tomorrow night". Billy got, up and staggered off to the bedroom. She could hear Billy, starting to snore. She sat down on the couch, and started to weep quietly, damning the all powerful karma and the fates. Armano sat at the table, the blonde beside him, and the two body guards. The blonde looked at the three, and said, "What are you waiting on? Johnny gave her a frightful stare. Armano gave Johnny a nod, shaking his head no at him. "There are people over there in those apartments who have a lead on were my my daughter is", Armano spoke quietly. The blonde just smiled, and stood still. Sirocco was making last minute plans before the blood moon rose. Bacalou returned with Glenda, dressed in some of Sirocco's wife's dead wife's clothes. "What the . . . he began. Bacalou, disguised as Jake, held up a hand. Glenda wore a mini-skirt, and tank top shirt, her breasts peeking out from it. "My plan is simple", Bacalou started, Glenda will deliver the plastic explosives on the courthouse, and the civic center at ten p.m. When the explosion comes, all the cops will be busy with that, and we can finish the ritual. ", he concluded. "Won't you baby', he grinned, producing his fork tongue, to tickle her ear. Sirocco looked at the two, disgusted, and then turned back to his reading. Erzule looked at the woman, Glenda. "If I could only reach her", she thought, maybe I can avoid a disaster, and free myself! Erzule concentrated hard on contacting Glenda, and whispered to the other one in her mind. "Sweet child, soon we will be free, your fate and mine will complete fate". In Erzule's mind, Angelica gave her thumbs up sign, and smiled. Erzule continued to try and probe Glenda's mind. Bacalou looked her way, with an evil grin on his face. Billy sat at the table drumming his fingers on it. Damn! He thought. I'd slept for two hours already. It was getting dark. Tomorrow night would be the final event, concluding the evil, or the good. Billy looked at Annie/ Marie. She was unusually quiet. Her early positive behavior had gone dark. Maybe she was preparing herself for the blood moon. Billy didn't know how to get ready for it. All he could trust at this point was good instincts. Billy tried to ignore his active imagination. Concentrated on checking his weapon, he ignored the bad thoughts that come streaming into his mind. Annie/ Marie sat on the couch, going into another trance. She was attempting to reach the voodoo child, and Erzule's mind. The block to communicating with Erzule, was slowly fading. Soon, she would be able to talk to her. Annie /Marie's forehead broke out in perspiration, dripping down on her shirt. She felt she was almost through. The block like red bricks, began eroding and crumbling one at a time. Annie/Marie was getting through, although slowly. She strained with all her power, then heard a voice. "Who are you? The voice asked, to interrupt me! Annie/Marie sent her an image of herself, then began to mentally hook up to the other mind. *"I am Marie Laveau, also in this mortal's body! She continued, Mama Erzule how can I help? The other voice paused, then said, "Come to me at the blood moon, just before midnight, the fates have arranged that! The voice continued, I must warn you.*. Then the voice trailed off. "What . . . what? Annie Marie asked, she was cut off by a blast of darkness, which rattled her head. "Shit! She yelled out loud in pain. Billy jumped up from the table, and ran over to her. He could see she was visibly shaken. "What is it?, he inquired, seeing her for the first time in this awful state. He had never seen such a traumatic reaction like this! She mumbled incoherently for a moment, and then spoke up. "I made contact with Erzule! She . . . warned me about something . . . some thing dangerous, and fate". She continued, "I think Bacalou threw me out of contact with her! "I could feel his darkness trying to overcome me! "What can we do? He asked. "It's in the hands of fate now, all we can do is follow it to the end". Billy sat with with her for a while, holding her close, comforting her.

# Chapter Fourteen

It was the night of the blood moon, which began at seven p.m. Bacalou packed Glenda's knapsack with at least Eighteen pounds of explosives. Bacalou had told Sirocco about the intrusion to Erzule's mind. Sirocco had filled up a syringe with five ccs of heroin, and injected it into the voodoo child and Erzule, which put her out for some time, hopefully. Bacalou looked at Glenda, admiring how she held up the heavy load slung over her back. "My girl ! He said, a little proudly. Sirocco stared at the two. "Go now! Bacalou commanded. Slowly she walked out the door, like sleepwalking., a step a time. She got into the vehicle, parked outside. Started it up, then drove off, a smile on her face. She drove fast to the courthouse. Erzule opened her eyes, slightly. Those fools hadn't realized the tolerance to the drug in Angelica's body. It had only knocked her out for maybe two hours. She closed her eyes, concentrated on gaining control of Glenda's brain. Her soul belonged to Bacalou, but she hoped there was one sparkle of humanity left, that she could appeal to. She began searching for Glenda's mind. Time would be running out son, and Erzule was doing her best to avert disaster. She opened up all channels to the air, looking. At the pizzeria, Armano was tensing up. He was getting ready for the blood moon. Soon, He thought. Glenda arrived at the courthouse. She looked around. The Navajo white of the structure stood out in the coming darkness. Twelve cement steps to the entrance were viewed. She saw one old man, a security guard, standing outside the entrance, catching a smoke break. He looked to be in his late sixties, early seventies. grey hair, growing long, peeked out of his uniform cap. He was slight of built, probably weighing in one thirty, soak and wet. Glenda smiled, this one will be easy to throw over. She quickly chose her options, and got out vehicle. The guard, Lew Mallory had retired from the police force fifteen years ago. Retirement sucks. His wife had died five years later, of ovarian cancer. Lew felt lost. He sat many a day, contemplating his demise. He had placed the old thirty eight revolver in his mouth several times, but couldn't muster up the courage to pull the trigger. Lew sat resigned to his inactions. Then a call! His old police chief, now retired, had called him. "Want a job? He asked Lew. Lew jumped at the chance, hoping it could keep him from unraveling his mind, at this point. Lew had agreed readily. The old police chief was in charge of security at the courthouse during the day. Lew was only to report suspicious activities around the area. Lew thought that would be great, an easy job. His arthritis was kicking his ass, and he had begun to drink heavily. Lew looked at the girl approaching him cautiously. "He kept his hands at his side, near his two way radio. Can I help you?,he asked her. She smiled at him, then said. "My husband has been dead for a while. "I went for a drive, to clear my head". I saw you standing there". "And ?, he asked her, wondering. 'I haven't had sex with a man in two years." She continued, "You look like a nice gentleman, and I thought . . . she paused, lifting her miniskirt up, revealing her blonde pubic hair that flashed before Lew's eyes. Lew swallowed hard, staring. Hell he thought, I'm old not dead. Why not! He may never get a chance like this again. It wasn't like women were beating down his door with offers she lowered her skirt, looking anxiously at him. "All right", he said, taking her hand, as they walked to the entrance. Lew's hands were shaking slightly as he fumbled with the keys, almost dropping them. "You ok honey, she asked, giving him her sexiest smile. Lew nodded, he said, we can go into the judge's chambers there's a nice big sofa in there, made of real leather". He smiled at her. She squeezed his hand, urging him on. They entered the judge's chambers, in darkness. He felt around for the light switch. Glenda placed her hand over his. "Never mind! She said to him, in louder voice. "I can guide you without the the lights, it's more fun that way. He looked at her doubtfully, then shrugged. Just as well, he thought, old age hadn't been kind to his body. She removed her top, revealing a wondrous sight of her breasts. She placed his trembling hands, on her breasts. "Hurry", she whispered urgently. Still trembling a little, Lew turned his back to her, and fumbled with his clothes. Glenda had stripped off her skirt, standing naked in the dark. Lew continued removing his clothes, slowly. Glenda had kept a curved blade hidden in her top. She slowly removed it. She stepped closer to Lew raising her blade. "Need some help, honey", she asked, raising the blade higher. Lew paused for a moment, then said, "I'm just about there", he replied to her, his back exposed to her. "So am I", she shouted, driving the blade in between Lew's shoulder blades. Lew jerked, trying to pull his pants up, and trying to reach behind his back. Fumbling, he fell against Glenda, and she and Lew tumbled to the ground. Lew attempted to remove the knife. Both parties grappled with the blade, as Lew pulled it out somehow. Blood gushed out on both. Glenda grabbed the knife, getting the blade in her hands, the hilt was pointed toward Lew, who had reversed the blade towards her. An inhuman roar filled her lungs. Lew hesitated. He was astonished at the animal noise she made. This gave Glenda the chance to grab the knife by the blade. Her hands now bloody from grasping for purchase with the blade. The two played tug of war with the knife. Glenda was losing, her hands slippery with her blood. Then she released the hold, using both hands to shove the old man away. Lew lost his grip too, and the knife paraded through the air, landing near Glenda. Winded, and hurt, Lew attempted to regain his balance. His staggerd. to stay upright, then felt the numbness in his left arm. A hell of a time to have a goddamn stroke.! He thought. Then gripping his arm, he tried to advance towards the woman, his hands clutched in rage. His body went numb, and his legs gave out. He collapsed onto the floor, aware but unable to move. Glenda brandished the knife in her hand, rubbing some of the blood onto her thigh. She hopped on top of the man sprawled on the floor. She didn't think twice on what to do. She leered into his face. Tough shit for you! And no pussy, forever! She cackled," This dance is over, goodbye ! She plunged the sharp blade into his eye, which gave a loud pop, then continued on into his brain. A sharp burning sensation filled him, then off to darkness. Sweet nothingness. Glenda paused to admire her work. Then with complete savagery she plunged the knife many times into his groin. "You won't be using that", she commented, and smiled. Looking herself over she was covered in some of her blood, and the old mans. She got up from the dead body, and looked around. She couldn't go to the civic center like this. She opened a side door, which revealed a sink and a shower. "That's what I call luxury", she said to herself. Turning on the shower, grabbing soap and shampoo, she began signing at the top of her voice. "What do you do with a drunken sailor", she sang on. After drying herself, she got out and retrieved her clothes, putting them on, she remembered leaving her knapsack on the steps. "Shit!she thought! Where is my brain! Then she smiled, gone of course! She rambled out to the courthouse steps, and retrieved it. She returned, went down the dark steps of the basement. There she found the boiler room. Inactive through the summer, a good place to park the explosives. She pushed half of them into the furnaces opening then closed. Laughing, she returned to the vehicle. Looking at a car approaching, she saw an elderly man, get out. Maintenance was written on the back of his blue work shirt. Humming, he went in, going down to the basement. The October weather was beginning to turn cold tonight. He better check the boiler, before old fart face the judge, would call him up complaining in his irritating, nasal tone. Asshole, the maintenance man thought. "Oh well, part of the job", he said to himself. He leaned over fumbling for the light switch. It was next to the staircase. He began descending the stairs, slowly. At seventy, he couldn't afford to fall and break a hip, let alone probably his neck too. He couched several times, then went to open the furnace door to inspect it. What the hell is that? He asked, looking at the plastic explosives. Then it dawned on him. A bomb! Oh shit, I need to get out of here. Moving too quickly, he reached the stairs, banging his shin,. He rubbed at the offending pain, then started to climb the stairs, two at a time. Glenda became anxious. What was he doing. She pulled out the detonator, and pushed the fire button. Just as the maintenance man made it to the top of the stairs, the furnace and the steps to upstairs roared, Flames shot out thirty feet in the air. Metal and glass, and wood spiraled up through the ceiling. It was no problem for the man, though. He had been cremated immediately, what remained went through the ceiling, cascading outward. Glenda grinned at the sight, as flames engulfed what was left of the building. Humming the tune she sang in the shower, she drove off slowly, heading for the Civic Center. She figured she had nine pounds of plastic left that should do it! Erzule strained all what left she had of her will power, trying to unblock Bacolod's influence on Glenda. The brick walls surrounding Glenda's' mind began to crumble into dust! Erzule brushed them to side, and entered Glenda's mind. It was a mess in there! Erzule began to clear the clutter up, remaining there. Then she was through, looking out through Glenda's eyes. She was too late to save the courthouse, but five hundred souls remained in danger at the civic center. She had to get through to Glenda, if a spark of humanity was still there. Erzule dug deeper into Glenda's brain. Looking through the files of her memory, she quickly sorted out what she could use, She transferred them, firing up them to Glenda. Glenda was heading to the civic center, almost there! She blinked tears as a pain shot through her brain, As if an ice pick was driven in there. The pain became intense, burning through whatever memories were there, and filled her up with new ones. Ones she had long buried within. She was almost there at the center, picking up speed. The soft memories of her past paraded through her mind. Her wedding day with McCarthy, their blissful honeymoon . . . The great sex, then. Then the birth of her son, Carl. Then she frowned, the crib death of him. No one could explain to her why. Anger began to fill her heart. It was replaced by a shimmering image of a grown man, his curly blonde hair tight on his head. Tall like her ex husband, and smiling affectionately. She knew in her mother's heart it was Carl! Mom, he spoke, his voice resounding in her head, 'Do not do this! "There are children there. If you remember your love for me, please don' kill them! "I'll see you soon! Glenda's tears over flowed her, soaking her shirt. She cried out, "I'll be with you too! She swerved the van away from the center, only missing the building she was aiming for. About forty yards. She had misjudged the acceleration she had built up. The van swerved from side to side, almost flipping over. On two wheels now, Glenda tried to gain control. At eighty miles an hour, it was defying the laws of gravity. The van flipped, end over end, and crashed into the police station. The last words Glenda spoke were, I'm coming to you, Carl. And then said, Thank God! She closed her eyes. The explosives had a delayed reaction. The van burning now, was going to touch off. Police on change of shift, scrambled out towards the van. Then the explosion! It rocked the station, Shards of metal from the van, and the concussive force of the bombs, flew high in a wide arc in the air. Ten police officers met their death, vanishing into nothing. McCarthy was blown back by the force of the blast, hitting the soda machine with his head. Dazed, he shook his head, and then got up, apparently only suffering a few scratches, and small abrasions. McCarthy looked around, assessing the damage. Pieces of furniture were scattered around, like some crazy unsolved jigsaw puzzle. Glass windows were totally shattered, leaving sharp jagged edges on the windows. Some of the flooring was gone completely, leaving a hole the size of a crater. McCarthy stood in shock. Then he spied Marlon's butt sticking out behind what was left of his desk. McCarthy grinned. "Come out from there, Marlon, it's over! Marlon crawled out, legs and butt first, sitting on the floor, just missing a widening hole next to him. "Holy shit, what happened? Marlon asked, getting up with his shaky legs. "Some asshole just blew the station up. Must have been a suicide bomber", McCarthy replied, his ears ringing from the concussion. Marlon was shaking his head too, trying to clear his ears of the impact; a bell sounding like the Hunchback of Notre Dame was ringing them. McCarthy began taking charge of the situation. He found a desk near him, with a phone. He heard the fire department ringing it's warning to the traffic. The phone rang surprising McCarthy. He picked it up, feeling a sense of apprehension. It was the chief. 'Oh, shit! He thought. The chief, Earl Simmons by name, roared into his ear, so bad McCarthy had to hold the phone away from his ears a few inches. "What the fuck is going on? He bellowed. Before McCarthy could reply, the chief continued his tirade. "Some asshole just blew up the courthouse, crap flying everywhere! Then McCarthy found his voice. "They got us too! he replied. What the . . . The chief began. McCarthy butted in, "A lot of casualties, and permanent damage to the station. The chief paused for a moment. "Jesus", he muttered. "You need to get this settled, or you're going back to patrolman. *Comprehede*! 'Yes chief. ", he replied. Hanging up the phone seething in frustration and anger. "Fucking desk jockey! He commented to the phone. He began dialing again, calling the CSI team, first, and then calling Billy. Billy answered the phone, dreading what was on the other end. McCarthy swore on the phone. "Damn it! He continued, 'All hell has broken out!" What is it? Asked Billy tensing up for bad news. 'Someone blew up the courthouse, and they got us too! McCarthy spoke, his voice rising in pitch. Oh shit! Billy said, looking at Annie/Marie. She looked at Billy, got up from the couch, and stepped over to him. Billy quickly relayed the message to her. "A diversion, she spoke, to get us from going to the factory." "The game is on! She continued, and we're behind. Billy gritted his teeth, "This shit ends tonight! He continued, Can you get away at eleven. We need your help". "I'll try anything as ling as it works", McCarthy said, then continued, "I'll back you up". With that McCarthy hung up. Billy said to her, "Tonight we put an end to this, no matter what comes! Annie/Marie sadly nodded. They checked their weapons, preparing for the upcoming battle. The age old conflict of good and evil would soon commence. Annie/

Marie gathered up all her magic, inhaling it in. Armano sat at the window, when the aftermath of the explosions hit them, shattering one of the windows in the pizzeria. The blonde shrieked, stepping back from him. "What the hell is that? He commented, brushing some stray glass from his suit. Johnny stepped out from the shop. A man and his woman brushed by him. Johnny reached out and grabbed the man, spinning him around. "What the . . . The man began, and then stopped, looking at Johnny's size. Johnny held him by his suit coat, and demanded, "What's going on? He shook the man a little. Johnny could almost hear the man's teeth rattle in his mouth. The man stuttered, cringing. "The whole damn world's gone crazy! The courthouse blew up! Then the police station! Johnny looked at the man, staring in amazement, His grip on the man loosened up. The man saw his chance and bolted away, as his woman stood, nervously by. He grabbed her hand, and took off like a bat out of hell. Johnny returned to the pizzeria. "Someone blew up the courthouse, and the police station! He exclaimed. "No great loss there", Armano commented. Then he smiled. "What that is a distraction to the police". He continued "I hope that those two cops don't get sidetracked by it! Johnny nodded, sitting down at the table. The three gangsters, and the blonde stared out the window, waiting. Billy and Annie/Marie were getting ready. Billy got into jeans, and a black t-shirt. Annie/ Marie was wearing the same, she had retrieved from her apartment. They looked at each other for a minute. They both looked nervously into each other's eyes. This was it! It was ten thirty now! Billy grabbed the phone, and called McCarthy. "It's happening", he told him. Billy gave him the address of the factory. McCarthy replied "I'll be there! I can't get anyone else, their all tied up with the explosion here! "Well bring who you can get, Billy said, then hung up the phone. McCarthy looked around. He saw Gregg come stumbling through the door, swaying. Hey, Gregg", he greeted the patrolman; "I need your help! Gregg staggering a little spoke up. "Sorry buddy, I don't think so". With a grin, He collapsed on the floor. Smoke rose up on the back of his uniform. A ten inch piece of rebar protruding out his back. "Oh, shit! He yelled, and then stepped over to check on Gregg. He felt for a pulse. Nothing, he was gone. A good friend for twenty years, they had graduated from the academy together. "Damn this! McCarthy said, almost on the verge of tears. McCarthy stood up, and looked around. Marlon stood there horrified at the scene. McCarthy slipped on his police windbreaker, and looked at the terrified I.T. guy. McCarthy checked his weapon. "Hey Marlon, he said to him. "Want to be a cop today, and go with me". Marlon snapped out of his trance. Marlon rolled his eyes, then said, "Hell yes". Even being gay, most of the guys had kidded him, but they all accepted Marlon. Gregg was a friend to him especially. "Here! McCarthy, reaching into his ankle holster and producing a 32 caliber pistol. Marlon looked at it, checked the clip, and returned it back to its chamber. "You know how to use that? McCarthy remarked. Marlon grinned at `him. "My father was an asshole, but he taught me how to fire any weapon. He continued, He was a marine drill sergeant for twenty years". Surprised at this, but didn't have time to mull that over, McCarthy just nodded. The two left in McCarthy's blue SUV. "Get ready for a wild ride; he said to Marlon, as they both buckled their seatbelts. McCarthy tore out of their in hurry, thinking thank god, the SUV wasn't damaged in the explosion! "That isn't any shit! Marlon quipped, making His boss smile. The two detectives got into the car, and sped off. It was eleven P.M. Armano saw them leave. "Let's go! he said to the two bodyguards. The blonde looked at him. Concerned. "I'll be back soon as I can, he squeezed her hand. "O.k., she replied. Armano knew he wouldn't be back, but felt he had to tell her something. The three raced to the car, and got in, leaving slowly away from the curb.

# Chapter Fifteen

Billy cruised around, waiting to see if McCarthy had caught up with them yet. Annie/Marie turned her head around to look also. Company's coming honey", she said to him. Billy turned to look at her. "Fuck them, he said, I know". "Let them", she stated, 'they are part of fate and karma in their plan. Billy looked at her puzzled, and then continued driving. Annie/Marie turned to turn on the radio. The announcer boomed, "And here's an oldie for you! The music blared out . . ." I am the God of Hellfire, and I bring you . . . Fire! The music boomed even louder. Smoke arose into flames from it! "Oh, *merde*", she said, trying to scoot away from the flames, undoing her seatbelt. Billy stared in disbelief, trying to stay on the road. Annie/Marie started chanting. Billy felt a warm wind flowing around him. Annie/Marie grunted. A clear protective bubble enclosed them. Billy reduced his speed. "Get out! he yelled to her, as they both tumbled out, hitting the ground. The protective bubble vanished, then. The car burst into flames scattering its bulk close to them. "Get down! Billy yelled into her ear, pushing her down into the soft patch of grass they were laying in. The metal flew, flying high into the air, like some crazy Roman candle. Annie/ Marie chanted again, and recovered the protective bubble around them. They could hear metal and burning debris bounce off the bubble, Billy could smell the acrid smoke in his nose. Johnny hit the brakes, several lengths from the wreckage. Several pieces of debris struck them, bouncing off, only damaging the roof a little. "Goddamnit", Johnny yelled hitting his brakes. Armano sat forward in the back seat." "We should pick them up", he suggested to Johnny. Then a siren resounded behind d them, followed by a blue SUV, following after it. Johnny pulled over to let them by. The three gangsters stared at it. The SUV pulled up to where Billy and Annie/ Marie stood up in the tall grass. It was McCarthy, and Marlon was with him! 'Get in, Hurry! Marlon yelled at them. Billy's ears were still ringing from the explosion. He knew so did Annie/Marie, shaking her head. Marlon pulled back the rear seat, and they stumbled in. "How's it going? Marlon asked. Hi fuck boy", she said to Marlon smiling. "I wish you'd stop saying that", he frowned at her. "Sorry", she said, looking into his eye. She continued, "I think you've had too much grief in your life already." Marlon started. "How would she know? He wondered. She reached out and grasped his right hand. A shiver went through his body. All the painful memories flashed before his eyes, and then vanished, leaving only a peaceful calm in his mind. She released his hand. "Today you will be remembered to all, she said to him quietly. "Never mind", Billy gasped, catching his breath. He continued, "Let's go, there isn't much time left". McCarthy just nodded, and floored the SUV, its engines roaring down the road. Johnny looked at Armano. "Aw shit! Armano said, "Follow them, I guess". Johnny kept a good distance between them, as he had switched with Gino. "We got company", McCarthy said looking in his rearview. "Yeah, I know", Billy replied. He continued, "The missing girl's father, that asshole, Armano". Billy continued further, "Let them follow us". Annie/Marie spoke up, nursing her foot, as she rubbed her left foot that had some abrasions on it. She had Removed her boot, and returned it back to hurt foot, wincing. She said, "They are part of fate and karma's plan". Marlon looked at her, giving her a strange look. McCarthy just grimly nodded. "Just believe her, she knows", he said to Marlon. Marlon just turned back around, staring straight ahead. They arrived at the old factory, and the four of them got out. They cautiously approached the entrance. Billy pulled out his pistol, and then looked at the other three. They all did Likewise. Billy leading the front, with Annie/Marie behind him. The other two, McCarthy flanked on the left, as Marlon flanked on the right. Annie/Marie stepped around Billy, and opened the door quietly. It squeaked a little, as the hinges were rusting some. She felt an aura of darkness emanating from the open door. She heard the human voice chanting, down below her. She looked at her watch, seeing it was eleven fifty! It was going to happen soon! The four crept down the rust metal stairs, trying to keep from making too much noise there. Annie/ Marie gazed down at the scene before her. A female body lay on the steel table. The man was hovering over it, chanting in an ancient Sumerian language. Then she saw it! Smirking its horrible presence, it's foul breath permeating the air. Its grey scaly skin stood out in the brightness of the room. The evil looking head had horns, sharp and barbed protruding from it. This was evil incarnate! "Bacalou", Annie/Marie whispered. She looked at the others, who stood dumbfounded, by the evil being! "Pure evil", she commented quietly, looking at them. "Looks like shit to me", Marlon said, a look of disgust on his face. He grinned nervously at her. The other two glared at him. Marlon closed his mouth tight. Outside, the gangsters pulled up behind McCarthy's SUV. All three got out, producing their weapons, ready for anything. They casually walked to the door. Annie/Marie spied the young girl chained by her hands to the wall. A pitiful sight. Looking filthy and tired, she gazed up at Annie/Marie. Their eyes locked. Erzule smiled, and then nodded her head. Annie/Marie stealthily crept down the stairs, closer to the girl, keeping an eye out for the human, and the beast. The two evil ones were concentrating on the incantation over the body. Annie/Marie got closer to the girl. Annie/Marie chanted some words over the loud chants from the other two. They still hadn't seen her! Billy crept down closer. He could barely make out the words she spoke. "Release this spirit from captivity", she announced spreading her hands in the air. The girl stirred, and began convulsing. Words spewed out her mouth "Free! I'm Free! I am Erzule, free from these chains. The chains gave a quick snap! Then disappeared into the air. A huge scream came out the mouth of the girl. A swirling mist exited her body, forming into the great spirit of Erzule. Her body glowed with a bright white light. Her adornments flowers surrounded her with red ruby jewels glittering on her hands, and toes. Sirocco looked up in shock! Bacalou growled evilly at her. It was midnight. The female on the table sat up, blinking her eyes. Sirocco looked at her tenderly. The voice spoke. Not of his beloved wife, but that of Harmonia, who's body he stole. "She will not come to you". She got up from the table, and spat on him. Sirocco stood still in shock as she approached him. She bellowed greatly at him. "She is safe with me! She abhors you! Sirocco screamed in despair! Bacalou reared up, giving a blood curdling roar. The beast grabbed her, and began tearing at her, body parts flying in the air, over the Bokar's shoulders. "NO! Damn you! Sirocco screamed at the beast. Sirocco attempted to separate the two. Shut up little man", Bacalou roared, striking a blow that sent the man flying. Sirocco quickly recovered, not out of the fight yet. Angelica came to, looking dazed. She shook her head, like waking from a deep sleep. She looked down at her body, covered in filth. "Damn! She exclaimed, realizing the chains were gone too. Annie/Marie touched the girl's shoulder. "Are you all right? She asked the girl. Angelica nodded, and then spied Sirocco. "Fucking bastard", she cried out. She grabbed the weapon from Annie/Marie, and running naked, ran towards the man who had imprisoned her. At that moment, Marie Laveau left Annie's body, turning into a fine gray mist. The mist turned to a fine gray mist. The mist spoke to Annie. "My quest is done. It's up to karma and fate now! The situation. She saw Angelica rushing towards Sirocco, her gun in her hand. Annie saw the girl raise the weapon, and cocked it back. But she didn't know Sirocco had kept a thirty eight strapped to his ankle. He fired once, hitting the girl between her breasts. Angelica screamed, drop the gun, and fell bleeding on the floor. Armano had entered the room, and saw his daughter collapse on the floor. The two body guards flanking him on both sides. "You fucking bastard! Armano screamed at the man, and fired one . . . two . . . Three rounds at the man. Two of them hit the man in the chest, and fell to the floor. Marlon creeping up on the left of Armano, thought he was firing at Billy, who was coming up to the left of the beast. Thinking his fellow officer was in trouble, Marlon made a quick decision. He blasted one shot of the thirty two, striking Armano in his throat, severing his carotid artery. Gasping from the blood squirting out of his neck, he fell to the floor. He slowly started to crawl to his daughter, the blood leaving a grisly trail behind him. Johnny and Gino shocked, empty their clips Into Marlon. His body hit the floor, riddled with ammo. Billy turned towards the two, as the same time McCarthy crept on them from the right. McCarthy fired first on the two gangsters. Gino fell to the ground, fatally shot. Johnny, still wounded, stood, still trying to reload his pistol. Billy moved forward, aiming his pistol at Johnny. Just do it", Johnny gasped, blood leaking from his chest, and arms. Billy fired point blank into Johnny's right eye. There was a whoosh of blood rushing out of his eye. His left eye seemed to glare at Billy, and then the gangster collapsed on the floor. Crawling slowly across the floor, Armano reached Angelica. A single tear fell from his eye. "I'm sorry", he gasped. A fine bright mist appeared over them. The faces of Magadena, and Maggie appeared. One voice spoke, "We will cherish her forever". The other voice concluded, "She will rest with us in nirvana". They enveloped Angelica's sprit, as she rose to be with them. They enveloped her, and then vanished. Armano smiled grimly, and then died. Erzule and Bacalou squared off, circling each other. "You will die now, bitch! He roared at her. He shouted defiantly at her, as the three who remained, stood mesmerized. "Dumballah! She exclaimed, "Come help your beloved wife". She chanted a short verse, and then backed away. Bacalou began moving towards her. "Today! She retorted to him, "You will return to the pit, where you belong! She began moving forwards to Bacalou. She grew ten inch nails on both hands, clacking them together, grinning at the beast. The air about them began to turn humid, and dark. The three detectives felt sweat breaking out on their bodies. A figure of a dark skinned man appeared, almost touching the ceiling. He was adorned with flashing jewelry, and bright flowers. "Your time to go is now", Dumballah roared at the beast, who began to backtrack fast. A look of terror sprang upon his face. Unnerved, Bacalou stopped for a moment. But full if his arrogance, and recent confidence, He sprang at Dumballah, like a leopard getting his prey. Dumballah laughed, as he met the evil ones attack. He grasped the beasts left arm, twisting it as he went. He began slowly spinning in a circle, With Bacalou in tow. Erzule moved forward, grasping the beast's right arm. They all spun in a circle, like some crazy out of control merry-go-round. They all began spinning faster, and faster, now blurring into a small tornado. The three survivors could hear Bacalou screaming for mercy. The tornado gathered up, faster and faster rising up through the air. The back draft from the wind pulled at the three, throwing dead bodies around, like some crazy Saturday cartoon. 'Let's get out of her! Annie yelled through the blasting air. They saw the dead bodies of Armano, the two body guards rise up, and Sirocco get sucked up into the whirlwind, then a sound of metal crunching was heard, resounding throughout the factory. The last thing the three observed was a jagged hole that had opened up in the ceiling. The tornado moved swiftly through the hole. Annie heard cries coming from it. The voices of the damned being delivered to their fate. Annie shrugged; goose bumps appeared on her skin. The three hustled as fast as they could to their vehicles. Billy and Annie jumped into Billy's car and spun out. McCarthy looked at them for and a minute, and then got in a fired up his car. As he turned to glance a last look at the factory, the building began to shimmer, as if it was a mirage. Then it began swirling around, like the tornado inside did. Then a large boom, concussing McCarthy's ears. He pulled over, his ears ringing like a school bell he heard as a child. He shook his head, trying to clear it. As he looked back, the factory had totally vanished! It left only a large crater in its place. Just like the factory never existed. What was it! He wondered. The voodoo gods or the hand of the almighty god, which destroyed it. McCarthy just shook his head; he had enough to deal with the chief, and giving an oral report to that asshole! His mind began to plan his summary. It was a voodoo cult that kidnapped the young girl. One of its members had set off the bombs in the courthouse, and police station. The four of them, Billy, Annie, Marlon and him tried to rescue the girl. The girl fought with the leader of the cult, and was killed. Marlon was killed trying to protect the other three. The factory had some faulty electrical wiring, which caused it to blow up. That was how he would submit his report. Keeping his fingers crossed, he hoped it would work out. His ex-wife was a victim of the cult brainwashing her into carrying out their deadly mission. McCarthy sighed, and then drove off. He turned on his radio. It began playing something about "Dirty deeds". He laughed hardily, as he felt a great weight lifted off his mind. "I think I deserve to get drunk", he said to himself, Maybe for a week! Billy and Annie arrived at his apartment. As they trudged up the stairs, Billy asked, "Is it over? Annie replied, "For now ", she replied. A worried look crossed her face as she remembered Marie's last words. What was it! Oh yes". Defying fate and karma, there is a price to pay! Annie discounted for now. Right now, she wanted to feel Billy's body close to hers. As they entered, Annie shut the door, and began stripping her clothes off. Billy stood still, admiring her body. Beautiful. He felt his second wind winding up. "Well? Annie asked him. Then she picked up her jeans, and removed the slave necklace from her pocket. "Am I going to have to use this? She asked faking menace in her voice. "Never! Billy laughed. He began taking off his clothes in the front room. They started off into the bedroom. Annie tossed the slave necklace on to the couch. Never know when I might need it! She thought. The bedroom door closed.

# Epilogue

**(Three months later} Annie stood at the grave site**, the grief and emotions drained out of her. She she knelt beside the marble monument. Billy Walker, born 1978March first—died January 16, 2016. McCarthy leaned over her, helping her up. Her legs were a little wobbling. "Let me help you up", he said quietly, offering his hand. Annie nodded, and then gained her feet. "If there anything I can do . . . he began. Anger gripped her, "The price you have to pay . . . entered her mind. Then she shook it off, and gave him a weak smile. "Thank you Mac", she said, "I'll be ok." "I'll drive you home", he said, helping Annie into his car. As he stopped at her apartment, she got out quickly, almost tearing the black dress of mourning. McCarthy looked distraught. "Are you sure . . . he began. Annie replied, "I'm fine Mac, see you". She leaned over and kissed his cheek. McCarthy gave her a forced smile, nodded then drove off. Annie went up the stairs to her apartment. Sadly, she sat down on her beige couch, the weight of her lost love bearing down on her. Then she opened up, crying non-stop. As she tried to stop the never ended flow of tears, a fine white mist began to form in front of her. It shimmered, than shaped into the figures of Erzule, and Marie. "What . . . Annie began the anger returning to her face. "Do not feel ill towards us, child, and Erzule spoke almost sympathetic. Annie just glared at the two. Marie chimed in; it was karma and fate that stepped in, not us! Annie just sat quietly. "WE wish to help you, like you helped us". Annie still didn't speak. "Here! Erzule pointed behind Annie. Annie turned her head to see another mist forming, shaping up into . . . Billy. There he stood still dressed in his funeral attire. Annie jumped up, and approached him. "Oh Billy! "I love you! She moaned. 'I will always be with you". He said, smiling. Erzule and Marie confronted her, moving as one. "We have defied the councils to bring him to you", Marie continued, with Erzule nodding. "He will be in your heart, forever! Erzule said, smiling. Pointing at Billy's image. It turned into a fine white mist that moved, and travelled straight into Annie's heart. Annie shivered, convulsed, then relaxed. She felt Billy's caring and love flowing through her. She smiled, and looked at the two spirits. Erzule said, 'You and Billy's fates are now together, entwined". "Be happy! Marie said, both spirits fading away. Annie was consumed with Billy, enjoying it. She turned to her mahogany desk, on the other side of the couch. She picked up a letter there, looking at it. She knew now that the car accident had been planned. It didn't matter, now. Billy will always be with her, until the end. She smiled at the letter. ""*Your appointment is approved as an investigative officer with The Kansa Bureau of investigation, in Topeka, Kansas.* Annie smiled and said to Billy, 'Are you ready for a road trip? She asked. No answer, but she knew deep down, he understood.

**Acknowledgments {Thanks to the following internet articles and books for their help. Hope I haven't inadvertently stepped on any toes)** 1. Michael Johnstone—The encyclopedia of spells 2. Magical protection by Amaris'Silver Moon 3. Voodoo image/ Shaman by Dreamtime.com 4. English/Sumerian language by Globe.com 5. Italian slang/ Curse words by Wikipedia free.com 6. Haitian/Creole language by Wikipedia free.com my humble thanks for the uses of these articles, and books to complete my novel.

Printed in the United States
By Bookmasters